Christmas Matters
A Covid Christmas Tale

Kennedy Rockefeller

DEDICATION

This book is dedicated to my Heavenly Father. You bless me so immensely, Lord. You are my very best friend.

This book is also dedicated to my husband, Taron. Thank you for being a tireless team member, a constant source of encouragement and a hilarious, awesome friend. Your amazing talent and phenomenal skill set has helped this dream come true.

CONTENTS

ACKNOWLEDGMENTS

To my mother, who chose life and who has always walked in utter godly grace.
To Mr. Stephen Brownfield, an English teacher who believed I was headed for great things.
To my five children, who supply me with daily humor, insight and love.

1

GETTING TO SNOW YOU

This year, Christmas was not the same. It simply wasn't. Kate hung the last stocking on her parents' fireplace and let out an exasperated sigh.

She had walked away from the cheerful scene in the kitchen, where her mother, Julia Hastings, had recently pulled a steaming pan of her butter-based, *sky-high* brownies from the oven. Heady swirls of chocolaty goodness wafted seductively through the air. Per tradition, the pan of fudgy decadence was bedecked with candy coated chocolates and brightly colored sprinkles. As her mom had placed the platter of fresh hot brownies on the kitchen table, Kate's father had let out a merry, "Ho, ho, ho!" In retrospect, *his* cheer may have been real exclamations of joy. The generous slope of her father's stomach provided ample evidence that the older gentleman enjoyed his sweets. But as for Kate, she felt close to nothing. Her small, "Yay," had been merely a performance for the sake of her mother, who made such a loving effort during holidays. Kate wanted to join into the cheer, but found herself overcome with an unsurmountable, unnamed, rather sad sense of..."*difference*."

Truthfully, everywhere she had gone people had been doing their best to be happy, hopeful. Essential workers everywhere--the grocery store, the bank, -- had all wished her a bright and bouncing, "Happy Holidays!" She had even spotted an ugly Rudolph themed sweater, complete with felt antlers and a blinking nose. People were being admirably brave, hugging one another warmly, trying to ignore the masks covering everyone's faces. The more cautious holiday-goers bumped or rubbed elbows affectionately, a careful gesture many were taking to "help the numbers go down."

Regardless, Kate felt so far away. She didn't want to believe that it was because of the stagnant, sad shape of her love life. It was easier to believe that it was because of the economy and overcrowded hospitals. No matter what it was, Kate wanted nothing more than to lay in her childhood bed, surrounded by old, worn out stuffed animals and music boxes too rusty to play. She'd recently discovered that a soft, quiet cry could feel quite healing during the winter.

In fact, she had only dragged herself out of bed and ventured to her favorite coffee shop because her sister, Beth, had *insisted* that she go. Beth had practically hauled her younger sister Kate by the arm and thrown her into Beth's small grey sedan. They drove to the shop with Beth preaching a small, but well-meaning sermon.

"I'm so serious," Beth started. "Max is stressed out. Hardly anybody is coming to the shop. She's fighting hard just to stay open." Beth strained to reach in the back seat while simultaneously throwing her car into park.

"If you care about small businesses," Beth continued, "now is the time to support them. Like it doesn't matter what you buy. Just get a pack of cookies. A piece of cake,--whatever."

Kate folded her hands thoughtfully and stared at the outside of the small, beloved shop. The waving Santa-bot was back, looking cheerful as ever. And this year, the top of the little coffee shop was decorated with white, Lucite fittings that made the shop look as if it had been thickly glazed by a sweet, mountain of snow-white frosting. Kate thought it was charming.

"Okay. Maybe, I'll just get something hot," she agreed quietly. "Covid can't survive above, what? Like 90° or something like that?"

 Beth shrugged. "Something like that."

"Then I'll get something hot, like a mocha caramel cappuccino. With marshmallows."

'Ooh, sounds good. Make it a venti!" Beth insisted. And with that, the two well-meaning ladies stepped carefully into the restaurant.

Back at the house, Kate sipped her cappuccino and milled wistfully around her family's living room. Hadn't it been just 12 months ago that she had stepped into this living room to celebrate this, her *favorite holiday*? Last year, she had strolled around feeling so carefree. At that point she and Derek were still together. Though not engaged, she felt that she and Derek had been quite serious. She had lost at least 15 pounds and was looking fabulous in her jeans. Mom and dad had been healthy. Her job as an account executive had been going well, so she'd had money to buy gifts for everybody that she knew. It had been a great Christmas. The strain between her and Derek had started when he began pushing against visiting her parents' house for the holiday. He thought he might want to travel instead, 'just the two of them.'

"And go where?" Kate had asked.

"Honestly, where doesn't really matter. But if I had to choose some place, I dunno, maybe Montego Bay?" he suggested. "Babe, have you ever been there?"

She greatly disliked him asking her that. He already knew she hadn't traveled much, despite her really wanting to. Contrarily, Derek had seen most of the globe, traveling with friends he knew from work and college. Derek was well spoken, well-traveled. Well dressed. Well....*everything*. His fudgy brown skin, chiseled features and well-defined pecs were all a part of his perfection.

"No, I haven't seen Montego Bay," she'd answered honestly, "But this is not the right time of year for that kind of trip. It's Christmas time!" she'd chirped. "This is *family* time. People get together, celebrate. Laugh. Eat ridiculous amounts of brownies and stuff like that."

"And get fat," Derek had countered. "I'm glad you shed some pounds. I was getting worried," he said.

Kate hadn't replied. It was so hard to have arguments with him. Something about Derek was very commanding. She nibbled subconsciously at her bottom lip and tried not to get emotional. Derek needed a strong person, she knew that. But he also didn't like women who talked back,or disagreed.

"Ok listen," she started, "We can do whatever you want after Christmas. New Year's, I'm all yours."

The discussion had been put on hold at that point. Derek had turned back to his closet and continued thumbing through his professionally dry-cleaned dress shirts.

New Year's, Kate had kept her promise. They'd sent pictures back from sunny Jamaica to her family. It amazed Kate that after stepping into the icy cold weather, she had been able to board an airplane, then disembark and stroll into a tropical, all-inclusive resort.
Truthfully, they'd had a phenomenal time in Montego Bay. Derek had insisted on flying first class, which was another thrilling first for Kate. While splashing in the Atlantic, she had donned a rather revealing bikini, *purple,* which was Derek's favorite color. They soaked themselves in the sun. Massaged their toes in the hot, pale sand along the beaches. Derek drank freely, flashing his premier black wrist band at every waiter on the property. Kate had followed suit, indulging in the cool, free flowing drinks, during what she feared might be a once in a lifetime vacation. She felt young, successful and sexy as she laughed and chatted with other young, fun-loving couples. It really had been a wonderful time. Though she normally spent New Year's cuddled near her mother's feet, she had no

regrets about going,--especially since Derek had been flexible about Christmas.

But after that vacation, their relationship had strangely fizzled. Awkward quietness became the norm. Text messages became few to none. Derek's visits to her apartment became rare. And when she called him, their conversations were polite. Perfunctory. Short.

By Valentine's Day, Kate felt that they were merely going through the motions. Derek had bought her chocolates and flowers. They were sitting on the front seat of his car when he'd picked her up. She'd slid into the passenger seat. Her timid, "Happy Valentine's Day," had been met with a casual, disinterested nod.

They'd had a meal at *his* favorite restaurant and ate without really talking. Kate spent the time examining her manicure and hands. Derek cared about all the little details and she didn't want to embarrass him by having chipped nails.

By Saint Patrick's Day, Kate feared that the relationship was pretty much over. Several people from the building had donned masks and traipsed over to a local bar to celebrate the Irish holiday. Kate suspected that Derek was already seeing someone else, most likely the shapely, aggressive brunette who worked as the office manager in Derek's department. A short, inebriated co-worker saw Kate standing alone and had tried to comfort Kate.

"Sure," he said, "Sheila and Derek have been working together a lot lately, as I'm sure you already know. But I don't think it's serious. I wouldn't worry about it."

Kate had never confronted Derek with her suspicion.

It was possible that he simply needed *"a break."* A chance to think about things. They had simply stopped texting, stopped calling each other. To any outsider, it would have seemed like a strange and weak end to a serious relationship that had lasted six months. But Kate, age 24, told herself that it was *fine.* That's just how things were now. You dated. You stopped dating. Maybe you pick up again later.

"Don't make a big deal about things," she said aloud. She comforted herself with thoughts that she was still young. She took a moment to stare into a large mirror-glazed ornament. Her small hands glazed over her hair. She had styled it perfectly, though she knew no one was coming. In her heart, Kate knew that the self-care and beauty treatments were small gestures she was making to just to help herself feel better. It was good to at least *look* put together. Even if, deep inside, you felt like a dirty gym sock. *Used and discarded.*

Graciously, upon her arrival, her parents hadn't inquired about Derek's whereabouts. Instead, her mother had abandoned all caution and threw her arms around her beautiful, youngest daughter, hugging her tightly. Kate was sure her sister, Beth, had let them know the situation, anyway. So, there was no need to fill them in on details

 Honestly, Beth was good that way. Sure, as kids Beth had been the older sister who would sit on you and shove snow in your mouth. Or spit in your chocolate milk. Or cut the feet off your favorite pink stockings. *"They were dirty. And stupid. Like you."* Beth had defended. However, all the slights paled in comparison to Beth's favorite dirty trick. The older sister made a holiday tradition out of finding a way to bite the sweet, rounded head off of Kate's gingerbread men, the *special ones* that their maternal grandmother shipped all the way from Arkansas. Kate loved the gingerbread men, and she knew that *no one else's grandma* made and shipped decorated gingerbread men all the way from Arkansas. She knew this because she had been sure to ask each and every other student in her third grade class.

As kids, Kate's tears had been mere gasoline on the fires of Beth's orneriness. So much so that she wondered if it wouldn't be a good idea to pay her back a little, and--

'Pingding-a-long!"

Clanging peals of her parents' Christmas themed doorbell chime rattled Kate immensely. As her hand shook from the surprise, she dropped her intensely hued lip gloss on the floor, breaking the fragile container.
Desperate to keep the gloss from staining the freshly shampooed carpet, Kate knelt quickly to pick up the container,--not realizing the small brick of wax had broken off its base. Her knee found the small bit of wax and smashed it deeply into her parents' cadet blue shag carpet.

"Who could that be?" She heard her mother ask.
"Kate, are you expecting someone?"
Her mother's voice was filled with curiosity, as well as a thrilled excitement she was trying hard to mask. Unexpected rings on the doorbell had been so rare over the past year. Neighbors weren't dropping by. No one was stopping in *"just to say hello."* If it wasn't a

delivery man frantically dropping off a package, you simply didn't hear the doorbell ring anymore.
"Kate?" Her mother called out again, seeing only the small arch of her daughter's back, as Kate was trying to rub the lip gloss stain off of her knee and out of her parents carpet with only the edge of her Rose Colored sweater.

"Merry Christmas!" exclaimed the surprise visitor. The deep, gravelly voice belonged to Jack Townsley, the owner of a small, construction company in the area. Though the company's work was constant and prolific during "construction season," things slowed down immensely during the winters. So, for years, Jack and his two sons ran a Christmas tree supply as well, providing premium trees to people who would settle for *nothing less than the best for Christmas.*

"Oh Jack!" Her mother exclaimed. "Bill look, it's Jack!" She exclaimed again. She couldn't see her mother, but Kate sensed the puppy like excitement her mother was feeling to have an unexpected guest. Her father came out of the kitchen quickly, straightening his pants as he did so. No one could ever accuse her father of shaking another man's hand while wearing droopy pants.

"That's pretty much a wrap for the season," Jack informed them. "We're not going to be able to move most of the rest. And I tell you what, we really got a beaut left out here." Jack paused to peek around the family's living room. "I didn't know if you folks had a tree yet, so we thought we'd share them with folks who've given us a little business over the years."

Kate's mother blushed. "Oh, we just used this old plastic thing this year," she explained, her tone sweetly apologetic."

Her father cut in to help. "Yeah, we just used Julie's mom's old tree. You know her mother died this past spring."

"Oh no, I didn't know that," Jack said, lowering his voice and folding his hands politely as a sign of condolence. "I'm sorry to hear that. But I tell you what, if you folks want this tree, you sure are welcome to it."

"Well sure," Kate's mom sang. But the sound of an oven timer in the kitchen, caused her mother to scurry away. "Kate, can you help your father?" She called over her shoulder.

"No need," Jake countered. " I've got these two boys out here. And you know they get cold if I don't work 'em hard enough." Jake chuckled at his own joke.

"Well here, I can help a little." And with that, her father stepped out into the cold with Jake, their neighbor. Kate used the moment to dash up the stairs in pursuit of a towel to wash lip gloss out of her parents' carpet.

Instead, she was blocked by her sister Beth who placed each of her hands on the opposite walls of the staircase, thereby successfully blocking Kate's way up the stairs.

"What's wrong with you? Beth asked

"Nothing!" Kate hissed. "Just get the heck out of my way. What's wrong with you?"

"Nothing." Beth stated, still blocking her sister. "Why are you in such a rush? And what's wrong with your face?"

Kate braced herself for whatever immature prank or stunt her sister was trying to pull. Blocking her way up the staircase was completely ridiculous. But now she felt as if her sister was playing a mind game on her. Beth was usually so awesome, but she had these moments...

"*Nothing's wrong with my face.*" Kate answered, acidly. "What's wrong with *your* face?"

"You mean you *want* your face to look like that?" Beth probed.

Kate didn't have time to answer. Her father's shoulder bumped their front door open. He came in grunting and panting carrying the tip end of a large tree.

Bill called out to his wife, as he coughed and gasped a bit. "Where do you want it, Julie?"

Upon seeing their father straining himself to carry the tree, both Kate and Beth sprang into action. Beth urged her dad to drop the leaden pine tree immediately, then settled her exerted father down in the kitchen, seating him and pouring him a glass of cool water.
Kate stepped awkwardly over the tree and began to assist Jack with carrying in the remains of the slaughtered pine tree. "Gimme a sec, Mr. Jack," she

grunted, while attempting to find a less prickly place to grasp the tree.

"It's Jim," a deep, gravelly voice corrected.

The sound of the strange, powerful voice caused Kate's head and body to pop up suddenly, like a prairie dog. The eyes she met were brown. No, *hazel*? *And sparkling*, she thought. *Definitely sparkling.* "Like warm crystal," she said aloud.

"Say what?" Jim asked. He leaned closer to hear the voice of the small blonde before him, despite the fact he was failing to don the appropriate PPE. He took a moment to look the small, shapely woman over. Her hair was very blonde. *Too perfectly blonde*, he thought. Her features were small and very pretty. Her eyes were sky blue. Bright. Innocent looking. *Very nice,* he thought.

"Oh bring it in, Dum-Dum."

Beth's sharp words broke the mutual gaze of the two entranced strangers.

"Right!" Kate almost shouted.

A loud blaring honk sounded outside. Jim's younger brother was leaning into the horn of their pick-up truck, mercilessly.

"Right," the man said. "Just tell me where you want it, then stand back six feet, if you don't mind."

"Over there," the sister's said simultaneously, and pointed to the space where a tired plastic, bedecked beast was already standing. The two ladies stood back, amazed as the virile young man, barely 27 years old, grasped the bulky, weighty tree and expertly swung and shifted the tree into place. The girls' heads turned in sync as they watched him dust off his powerful thighs and take three authoritative steps toward their front door.

Jim gestured toward the tree and spoke with the strong, unapologetic tone of a foreman. "Keep it watered. Keep it away from flame. Secure it. *Please*,"

Without meaning to, Jim and Kate allowed their gazes to interlock. The electric, instant spark of connection wasn't lost on Beth. With the well-meaning spirit of an older sister, Beth gently nodded her head toward Kate.

"She's single, you know," Beth stated.

"Oh my Lord!" Kate spurted out. "I am already. I mean, I have the...Derek..." Her voice dropped off as her brain froze from humiliation.

"He hasn't called for *months*," Beth countered. "I'm pretty sure it's over." Her attention turned back to Jim. "He doesn't even text her anymore. She's totally single." Beth finished.

Jim smiled his crooked, winning smile. Kate noticed the fiery glimmer of light that played along the edges of his amber eyes.

"Good to know," said Jim, still smiling. His mood changed very suddenly however, as his ground his fist into the horn, blasting.

"Alright already!" Jim barked out, then turning back to the two sisters standing mutely in the living room, he smiled again and nodded politely. "Nice, to meet you, ladies.".And with that, he strolled off and joined his scowling younger brother.

As the truck pulled out of sight, Beth strained to watch the vehicle disappear down the road. "*Townsley Construction*," she said aloud, recalling the name printed on the side of the pickup. She took a breath, then opined, "Boy, was he good-looking. I liked his eyebrows. Did you notice his eyebrows?" she asked. Beth turned around slowly, searching for a reply, only to realize that she was talking to herself.

Her sister Kate had dashed away, having remembered her mission to scrub the lip gloss out of her parents' carpet. Unfortunately, as she peeked around her parents' upstairs bathroom, she caught a glimpse of her face in the mirror. She stood there for a moment, mortified. Is this what she had looked like when she'd met the handsome stranger?

"What's wrong with your face?" Beth had asked.

And now she knew why. In addition to having bright red lip gloss ground into her the knees of her light blue jeans, the gloss was also smeared into the edge of her sweater and staining her hands. Worst of all, the pretty crimson lip gloss had made a strange line of color that stretched from the edge of her mouth to the apple of her right cheek. It was only an inch or so. It looked almost like a checkmark. She realized it must have happened when her hand shook at the sound of the doorbell. Half-amused, she snorted a little at the way that she looked. This really was just going to be the *worst* Christmas ever, she realized. That thought made her want to laugh and cry at the same time.

...But the stranger, Jim, when he'd looked at her, he had simply looked her straight in the eyes. He hadn't looked revolted or disappointed. It was almost as if he hadn't even noticed her slightly Joker-like lip gloss. "Of course, he noticed," she said aloud, correcting her own thoughts. "That's the stuff men care about." Kate snatched a small, dark green rag from beneath her parents counter, and let the door of the cabinet close loudly.

2
TREES A CROWD

The next day Kate awoke to the sound of muffled voices downstairs. She didn't feel like moving right away, even though she didn't recognize all of the voices, her curiosity was starting to be piqued. It was strange how comfortable sleeping in her old bedroom could be. Unsurprisingly, her mother had kept her room largely the same. The small difference? Boxes of crafting supplies and scrapbooking materials now filled the corners of the bedroom.
Kate stretched and sniffed the air. She wasn't certain but she thought she could smell more fresh brownies being baked. As she glanced about, she thought that the walls glowed pinker than what she remembered. The shade was called "Candy Town." Too pink for her adult taste now, she felt, but still quite sweet.

"She's just upstairs," she heard her mother say before Julia's voice rang out with a clamoring, "Kaaate!"

Even though she was awake, her mother's glass-shattering scream kick-started Kate's pulse. Had she been close to the edge of the bed, she was sure she would have fallen out. Kate cocooned herself in the ancient, magenta comforter she had been sleeping under and walked toward her door. Upon opening it, her sister's face jumped forward suddenly, unexpectedly.

"Guess who's here." Beth whispered excitedly, her face mask hooked beneath her chin.

Kate huffed dramatically, unpleased about being startled so much first thing in the morning. "Lemme guess. Santa?" Kate sneered.

"Screw Santa," Beth huffed. "He's married and he's old. No, *Jim.*"

And with that announcement, Beth grabbed her little sister by the shoulders and pushed her into the hallway so she could get a better look at the handsome stranger standing by the front door.

Kate gasped audibly and clamored to get back into the safety of her bedroom. "What is *he* doing here?" Kate demanded, her words loaded with accusation.

"I called him," Beth confessed, laughing as she did so. "It wasn't hard. The number was online, so I called his dad's company, *Townsley Construction.* When I called, the system said to push 'number one' for Jack, or 'two' for James. I pushed 'two!'" Beth's hands were shaking excitedly as she admitted her actions.

"But why?" Kate inquired, though she was afraid to hear her sister's next words.

Beth's eyes narrowed, almost accusationally. "Are you kidding me?" She hissed. "When you two met in the living room last night, it was almost electric. You couldn't take your *eyes* off each other." Beth moved away from her sister and searched around the room. "Now. Don't you have something hot you could put on quickly? Something glittery? Something tight? Kinda sexy?"

"Sure," Kate started. "Just lift Grandma's old hymnal on the table over there, and you'll find my pair of crotchless fishnet stockings."

"Oh good," her sister answered, failing to detect her sister's sarcasm.

"Morning, sweetie!"

Kate swung around to see her mother standing in her bedroom.

"Kate, honey, that nice young man who dropped off the tree yesterday is here. He said you called and left a message asking for him to come and change out the tree." Julia's face twisted into a slightly confused, slightly disapproving glance, but she said nothing further.

Kate drew back, surprised by her mother's words. "Wait a minute, he said that *I* called?"

Beth moved forward, "Well, I couldn't say it was *me*. Here, put this on."

Kate held up the article of clothing her sister had shoved into her hand. It was a neon pink, sequined covered leotard, a hideous reminder of Kate's time on her high school's dance team.

"Ha! I don't think so." Kate objected.

"It really does look nice on you," her mother plied. "Plus I haven't seen you wear it in forever." Julia clucked her tongue. "Do you think you can still fit it?"

"Oh I can fit it," Kate said, attempting to hide her slight offence at the suggestion that she had put on weight since her high school days. "But unless there's a school pep rally tonight, I hardly see how this is the right get-up."

"Just put it on," Beth ordered, gently. Turning to their mother, Beth cooed, "Mom, can you offer Jim a brownie or something? One of your world class brownies? Or some tea?"

"Oh I should. Good idea, baby girl," her mother agreed, though she hated to step away right at that moment.. She could sense that fervent, romantic plotting was taking place, and she would have very much enjoyed co-plotting with Beth. Instead, chuckling quietly, she left with, " I'll leave you two girls to it. See you downstairs. Be quick!"

At the disappearance of their mother, Beth's head turned slowly back to Kate.

"Look Dum Dum, I've got a *really* good feeling about this guy. Went through the whole trouble of concocting this little snow job just to get him here for *you*." Then, with visible aggravation, Beth added, "Besides, Derek was a butthole. Shallow. Rude. Just like every other guy you've dated since middle school."

Kate rolled her eyes and tossed the pink leotard on the bed. Her sister's words stung, and she believed them to be untrue. *Hoped* them to be untrue.

Noting that her chosen article of clothing had been rejected, Beth raised an eyebrow threateningly. "Look, the guy is *waiting* for you downstairs as we speak. Just put on that leotard and a nice pair of jeans, then go downstairs and say hello."

Kate huffed, unsure that she felt up to socializing. She felt doubly unsure about being *jammed together* with a practical stranger via Beth's half-concocted plan.

Sensing her sister's hesitance, Beth added, "And if you don't come down, *immediately*," she started, menacingly. "I've got enough embarrassing and humiliating photos on this phone to keep him entertained for *hours*."

Kate snorted and rolled her eyes. She folded her arms in obstinate defiance of her older sibling's threat, even as Beth began to thumb through the photos saved on her phone.

"Here's a nice one from Jamaica," Beth warned, her voice oily with intimidation. "Great boob shot."

Kate grabbed her sister's hand and stared wide eyed at the pic of herself splayed out on a hotel room bed, her left nipple peeking from behind her colorful sundress.

"How did you get that? Who took that picture?" Kate demanded as she steadily tried to pry the phone from her sister's hands.

Beth, though slightly shorter than her younger sister, was quite skilled at fending off Kate's maneuvers. Beth read, "The caption reads, 'Kate after 3 mojitos and a tequila shot.' "

Kate's eyes closed slowly, resignedly. "Derek,..." she moaned.

"Leotard. Tight jeans. Cute boots. You've got less than *one* minute," Beth commanded. And with that the older sister whooshed out of the room and trotted down the stairs to stall the polite, muscular man waiting for her sister.

Minutes later, Kate found herself riding along beside the handsome stranger, Jim, in his company's surprising luxurious pickup truck.

"I figured we may as well let you pick out the tree you actually want," he said. "I didn't want to do any guess work this time. End up getting the wrong one."

Kate blushed beneath her mask. It was one of the best things about wearing a mask. It hid her habit of nervously biting her lip, as well as her tendency to blush.

"I promise you, it doesn't really matter to me," she insisted. "Any tree is fine."

Jim laughed quietly. "Well, you've sure changed your tune. I believe your message said something along the lines of the tree we gave you being 'scraggly?' "

"Ha, no I wouldn't have said that." Kate rebutted.

"Or did you say 'spindly'?" Jim wondered aloud.

"No I--"

"You definitely used the term "ghetto," Jim recounted.

"Not once in my life have I used that term!" Kate growled, distressed to think of what else her sister may have said in her message to Jim,--all due to Beth's *desperate* effort to have the potentially eligible young man return.

Jim turned to look at the perky blonde beside him. Her blue eyes were even more noticeable with her lower half of her face covered.

"Where'd you get that mask?" Jim asked, his tone light but mildly sarcastic.

Subconsciously, Kate touched the fuzzy purple mask stretched across her face. In the quiet, boring first days of the quarantine, her mother had sewn masks for the family. The masks were cute. Well, *cute enough* anyway. Kate hadn't planned on wearing her mask anywhere but around her parents house. She would have chosen a more sensible mask to wear on this errand. But Beth had shoved Kate out of the front door, jammed the purple velour mask into Kate's hand, then shut the front door soundly in Kate's face.

"I mean, I guess it's better than *nothing*," Jim gibed, sounding more critical to Kate than he meant to sound. "It's just *really* purple. And kinda silly."

Kate turned her attention away from the driver and looked out of the window. His criticism perturbed her. She retorted, "And where's your mask, may I ask?"

Jim's eyebrow raised slightly at the sound of Kate's testy tone. He didn't answer right away, but he was a little amused at the perky blonde's irritation. He'd only teased her a little about her mask. He didn't expect for her to get annoyed with him. Honestly, he thought the mask was cute. It totally fit her. Fun, flirty. Though he hardly knew her, Jim had pegged Kate as the kind of girl who would have been a cheerleader in high school. In his mind's eyes, he could just see Kate standing in a high school gymnasium, furiously swishing jumbo sized pom-poms, her shiny blonde hair reflecting the glare of the lights. As she shouted some nonsensical, peppy cheer, he would have stared at her from the bleachers, wide-eyed, adoringly.

Though smart, Jim had never been a stand out student himself. At times, he believed that, had he invested himself into high school a little more, he could have done better than secure the foreman's position at his own father's company. He had been a decent hockey player. Could have turned into something? Regardless, from the young age of 16, Jim had already determined his occupational future. His father Jack had built the company from scratch. Jim believed that it would be best to simply take over his dad's company one day. That plan had a sense of legacy and tradition that appealed to him. He made a comfortable enough living for now, especially around Christmas time when people swallowed up Christmas trees like candy.

"And it's actually pretty breathable," he heard Kate say, pulling him from his reverie. When he looked over, he noticed Kate's eyes seemed to be flashing with a displeased fire.

Jim smiled and nodded, but chose not to reply. They continued to drive in tense silence for a few minutes more. Then, taking advantage of a red light, Jim strained to reach the button to his glove box.

"Hand me that right there," he said, pointing to a piece of fabric in the glove box.

Kate obliged, and in seconds Jim was wearing a black polyester face mask. The words "Merry Christmas!" And "Happy Holidays!" lit up intermittently and scrolled across his jet black mask.

Kate snickered at the silliness of the mask, despite herself. It seemed a bit too lighthearted and playful to be something that her companion would have chosen for himself. "Let me guess," she ventured. "Your mom?"

Jim pulled carefully into his family's lot of trees. "We're here," he announced. "Come on out and pick whichever tree you like. I'll take it back to your parent's house and haul away that other one. *For free.* Okay?"

Kate's eyes searched the face of the man she was sitting beside. She looked for signs of irritation or anger in his features. Finding none, she felt relieved. Having him out like this, under such false pretenses, gave Kate sudden pangs of guilt. "Tell you what," she started, "I'll pick out a tree, and *yes* it'll be nice of you to take it back to my parents' house. But you'll have to let me pay for it. For the inconvenience."

Jim raised an eyebrow and glanced over the woman sitting in his passenger seat. He appreciated her offer, but thought of a better idea.

"Nah," he said. "Not looking to take your money. Dad wanted your family to have a nice tree. And he's giving it to you guys. It's not a big deal." Jim pulled on some work gloves and started to open his door. Looking back over his shoulder, he offered, "But I tell you what, maybe you could buy me a hot cup of coffee on the way back to your parents house."

Kate smiled, thinking Max would be delighted to have even more of her business.

"I know a *great* little coffee shop," she said.

An hour or so later, the attractive pair of new friends stepped confidently into Max's Coffee Shop.

"Max!" Kate called out, cheerfully. "Back again. And this time I've brought a new friend."

"Oh, awesome!" Max replied, wiping her hands on a striped dishcloth. Max's red hair was pulled back and gathered into an uncareful ponytail. True to form, she was wearing a man's red plaid shirt and ancient, tight fitting blue jeans.

"This is Jim," Kate informed her. "I don't know if you know his dad, Jack Townsley?"

Max nodded dutifully, hoping her customers would settle in for a while and order hundreds of dollars worth of coffee.

Turning her attention to the menu, Kate mused. "Let's see what I want…"

Jim glanced over the menu board as well, but needing a bit of a breath, he pulled his mask down for just an instant before replacing it over his face.

"Wait, I know you," they heard Max think aloud. "You run the Christmas tree lot out near Wildwood?"

"Yeah," Jim answered excitedly, surprised to be spotted and recognized. "That's my dad's place. I help him run it. It'll be my place, eventually," he informed her, realizing that he had mentioned the latter fact in an attempt to impress the pretty redhead.

"That's the only place my aunt will ever get her trees," Max shared. "Like, she drives out there *every* year. We used to ride with her. She swears those trees last twice as long as anyone else's. As if it matters."

Jim laughed, "Right. All the trees will be garbage a week after Christmas."

Kate glanced over, taking note of the easy, free-flowing chatter happening between the two strangers.

"No offense, but I don't even think I'm going to put up a tree in my apartment this year," Max said, shaking her head as she considered it. "I'm half Jewish anyway. I should just put up a menorah and be done. It would be so much cheaper."

Jim nodded, "Do it. I mean I think people make too big of a deal out of Christmas, anyway. Saving money is smart, especially right now."

Kate stood still, stiffened with apprehension and an emerging sense of competitiveness. Though she'd only known Jim for a short while, she felt a strange ownership over the single man. The flow of conversation between Jim and the shop owner seemed so effortless, so natural. Envy-based feelings urged her to disrupt their connection.

"Did you cook anything today?" Kate asked.

Max turned her attention to her long-time customer. "Yeah, Sweetie. Always. What would you like?"

"Maybe some soup," Kate suggested, then noticing that the pretty shopkeeper's board looked incomplete, Kate probed, "What's *supposed* to be the soup du jour?"

Max rolled her eyes. "I dunno. I haven't even looked at my own menu," she admitted. To Kate's disdain, Max's candor caused Jim to laugh. He looked even more amused as the height-challenged red-head yanked a step stool from behind her counter, then used it to jump and twist herself around enough to view her own menu board.

"Chicken noodle," Max informed her. Then, detecting a bit of disappointment on Kate's face, Max added,

"With all-you-can-eat crackers!"

"Oh, I'll take some of that," Jim erupted, nodding and smiling eagerly. "Sounds good. And a black coffee, too."

"Okay, I'll take the soup, too. And the Cuban panini. And a low fat, sugar free mocha cappuccino with double foam," Kate insisted. Truthfully, she was hungry. But more than anything, she realized that she wanted to keep the shopkeeper busy for a while in the back of the kitchen,--*out of Jim's sight.*

Having placed their orders, Kate bumped Jim's elbow with her own, and motioned him over to a table situated *several meters away* from Max's counter.

Once seated, Kate pulled off her cable-knit cap and unwrapped her scarf from around her neck, attempting to use smooth elegant motions as she did so.

Looking across the table at her striking new friend, she touched her face mask gently and asked, "Mind if I take this off?"

Jim stiffened a little. His feelings about masks were inconsistent. While he didn't enjoy wearing one, he preferred when others left theirs on. A moment or so after she asked for permission to remove her mask, he realized that he was still wearing his own, and that his mask had been sparkling with colorful LED lights as he had chatted with the pretty shop owner.

"No, go on," he offered. And after she did so, Jim enjoyed the chance to see the uninterrupted view of the slim, pretty face of the woman before him.

"Now you," she toyed, playfully.

Without ceremony, Jim ripped off his mask and slapped it down unto the table. "Probably doesn't help keep us safe anyway," he mused aloud.

Kate didn't answer, unwilling to venture into debate. "Well you look very handsome with or without it," she flirted boldly.

"Oh...wow, thanks." Jim chuckled loudly, nervously. Though sincerely attractive, he had never gotten used to compliments from women. Compliments excited him, enticed him, but they never happened with enough regularity for him to actually get *accustomed* to them.

He sat forward and leaned the smallest bit across the table. "You know, the other day when I dropped by your parents house. I noticed your eyes were blue."

"Yeah they are," Kate agreed, blinking dramatically for effect, a trick she had learned from a "How to Flirt Video" she had seen online.

"Is that sky blue or cadet blue?" Jim asked her. "What would you call it?"

Kate smiled a charming smile, hoping the small dimple in her right cheek was showing.

"Baby blue," she informed him with a very certain nod of her head. "I got voted "Best Eyes" in high school. Everyone agreed that they were 'baby blue.' " Upon sharing this detail about herself, she felt a bit silly. People over the age of 21 shouldn't brag about things that happened in high school, she thought. It sounded so immature.

The inappropriateness of the comment was lost on Jim. "Baby blue," he rasped, sounding almost entranced as he stared into her eyes.
Kate stared back, looking deeply into Jim's amber colored eyes. In the low light of the coffee shop, his eyes looked more deeply brown, more like honey-glazed chocolate. Not the fiery amber they had appeared to be in light of her parent's home, but still gorgeous and alluring all the same.

Jim's words broke the sweet silence between them. "I hope you don't mind my asking, since we just met" Jim started, "But are you seeing anyb--"

"Here you go!" Max sang, delivering herself and the food to her customers. She staged the loaded platters at a neighboring table and brought each dish over individually, carefully sliding the entree's before Jim and Kate. Each time she turned around, Kate couldn't help but notice how shapely and toned the shop owner's backside appeared to be in her skin-tight jeans. Jim's eyes seemed to have made the same discovery, though he forced himself to look away from Max's alluring curves once he caught himself staring at her figure.

"Alright guys, enjoy!" Max bubbled. However, instead of stepping away and allowing her customers to eat their meal in peace, Max stood by their table, as if waiting for something, though Kate couldn't imagine what.

Jim leaned his face toward the steaming food, enjoying the aroma of the treats before him. "Looks great," he offered, smiling appreciatively at the woman who had prepared them.

Max returned Jim's smile. Pointing to the soup she had merely reheated, she shared, "That soup, that's my grandmother's recipe. That's been in the family for like, a thousand years."

Kate chortled, derisively. "That's ridiculous."

"No seriously," Max defended. "My great, great grandfather brought it with him from Scotland."

"So you're Scottish," Jim observed, excitedly. "That explains the red hair."

"I know, I'm a total ginger!" Max conceded, taking the opportunity to entwine both of her hands in her mass of red tendrils. "Do you hate red hair?" she cooed.

"No, not at all. It looks good," Jim said, then after taking a moment to swallow, he added, "*Really* good."

Kate turned to view Jim's face. His eyes appeared to be dancing all over Max's face and hair. To Kate, he seemed practically enraptured. Attempting to break the mild spell that the '*ginger*' was casting over her new beau, Kate cleared her throat audibly, and demurred,

"No, I like it, too." She quickly added, "And the food looks really good. So...we're just going to *eat it now*." Kate twirled her spoon expectantly, allowing the utensil to hover impatiently just above her soup.

"Right!" Max, exclaimed, slapping her carrying tray against her thigh. "I'll just let you two..."

Max's words trailed off as she stepped to a nearby table and brushed off imaginary crumbs.

However, Jim, seeing that the friendly young woman was merely walking away toward the lonely, unbusy counter, countered with, "Or you could just pull up a seat and chat with us." With that, he pulled a third chair up to their table and motioned gently to the seat.

Kate felt her eyes rolling to the back of her head as Max slid into the seat. Max's smile seemed genuinely charmed as she settled herself close to Jim. Suddenly, in one fell swoop, Max's hair was unleashed from her ponytail and bright red locks cascaded freely around her shoulders and face.

Kate eyed Jim's response as he watched Max's beauty unfold before him. The gentle gulping motion of his adam's apple wasn't lost on either woman.

Feeling suddenly warmer, Jim removed his coat and draped it on the seat to his left.

Eyeing Jim's physique, his apparel caught Max's attention even more. "Oh my gosh, is that a BLM shirt?" she chirped.

"Yeah, a friend gave it to me," Jim answered carefully, not wanting to spark a disagreement between himself and the crimson haired beauty.

"Oh my gosh, look!" Max started. She disrobed quickly, ripping open her flannel shirt and revealing a sleeveless, cropped "Black Lives Matter" t-shirt.

Kate eyed the political shirt, and the exposed midriff of the shop owner. The skin of her stomach looked velvety, smooth and flawless. Her belly ring, lined with multicolored beads, looked shiny and playful,

Jim's appreciation of the red head was no longer masked. His eyes roamed all over the short, shapely, politically active shop owner.

"Oh my gosh," Kate chirped loudly, imitating Max, "I didn't know the BLM made belly shirts."

Max laughed loudly at Kate's comment, lounging forward as she did so. The small movement set Max's full, braless breasts into motion. The erotic, feminine jiggle did not evade Jim's observation. His eyes were wide with delighted appreciation.

"No, I cut it myself," Max admitted. "It would just get so hot out there. During the demonstrations."

"Oh wow, you *marched*?" Jim inquired, his voice ripe with admiration.

"I did." Max nodded in full approval of her actions. "I just couldn't see standing by and doing *nothing*. I have *friends of color*," Max stated proudly. "I might even have a cousin who's half Black, I think."

"Oh well…if you *might* have a *cousin*…"Kate quipped, feeling largely invisible. Her words, however, did *not* go unnoticed. Both Max and Jim turned their full attention in Kate's direction.

"Did you march, Kate, or go to any of the demonstrations?" Max questioned.

Kate blushed a bit at the direct question. Though embarrassed by her answer, she shook her head proudly. "I was dating someone *pretty seriously* at the time, and he was really afraid I'd be hurt."

Jim nodded, satisfied by the answer. A naturally protective person himself, he found Kate's explanation sufficient.

Max, however, felt urged to prompt further. Tilting her head like a curious cat, she probed, "Oh, so… then why didn't he just go with you? To *protect* you?"

Instead of answering, Kate took a deliberately large bite of her sandwich and began chewing animatedly. For Kate, it was so hard to have these conversations with friends or family. Or neighbors. Or shopkeepers. Kate felt herself to be a deeply compassionate person. She cared about everyone around her. But so often, the men she dated were staunchly "Back the Blue" right-wingers. Not bad guys, she felt. Just straight up and down conservative types. She was drawn to them, and they were drawn to her. She couldn't even say why it was that way.

Max pushed further with, "I mean, I just can't see *myself* dating the kind of person who would try to stop me from standing up for what I believe in."

Jim nodded respectfully, admiring the redhead's zeal and passion.

Kate finished her bite and considered her next words carefully. "Well," she started confidently, feeling suddenly determined to state her own feelings clearly. Except, instead of providing her with solid, logical reasoning, her brain froze completely. Her mind went absolutely blank, even as she searched desperately to find the words to express her sentiments regarding issues that she, too, believed to be important.

"Well," Kate started again, now feeling more like a malfunctioning car whose ignition failed to engage, no matter how many times she turned the key.

In the middle of this increasingly awkward discourse, Max's sense of customer service re-emerged.

"Well," Max began, "You know, we're all different. And each person has the right to feel however they *choose* to feel...I suppose."

"Absolutely!" Kate shouted, her overly loud words bouncing off of the empty shop's brick walls. Then, her brain suddenly recalling a random political statement she had heard a previous boyfriend share, Kate pronounced, "Besides, not all Black people are innocent."

Kate watched as Jim's soup laden spoon stopped in mid-air. She continued, "And cops work really hard. But no one ever worries about them. But they're the ones who keep us all safe."

Kate's view turned upward as she watched Max's mouth become increasingly agape. In truth, Kate wasn't even sure if the thoughts she was sharing were her own. Were they her thoughts, or were they just so deeply embedded into her psyche because she had heard them so often? She reassured herself, believing that even if such a disturbing notion could be true of herself, it could very well be true of everyone.

For a few awkward seconds the cafe resonated with silence. It was the strained, dangerous silence that often emerges when friends of different viewpoints attempt to speak about controversial, politically spring-loaded topics. They each feared that there was nothing to say to break the tension. No way to calm the waves. And yet, Kate spoke again.

"*All lives matter...*" she practically sang, Kate's voice and words sounding strange to her own ears.

The ride to her parents house had been strangely quiet.

At the cafe, Jim had neither supported nor condemned Kate's words. Kate had spent the time staring out of the pick-up truck's mud speckled windows, trying to forget the humiliating scene at Max's. As they drove, the local lanes were duly festive with multiple homes draped with colorful blinking lights. Even businesses and banks had wreaths or lights twinkling. Shopping plazas looked perfectly pleasant with their signs alighted, each featuring latticed fruit pies, toys that hummed or buzzed, and juicy, glazed hams.

"What's your favorite kind of pie?" Kate had asked, hoping to coax Jim into talking and lightening the mood in the vehicle.

Jim hadn't responded. In fact, he had inadvertently turned on his radio at the exact same moment Kate had posed her question. She didn't repeat herself. At the moment, a little holiday music seemed even better than forcing cheer and conversation.

Upon entering their home, Kate marched solemnly and quietly up the stairs to her old bedroom. She left it to her sister, Beth, plus Jim and her parents to complete the *completely unnecessary* tree exchange. Several minutes later, Kate heard a careful knocking at her door. She didn't bother to answer. She hadn't realized that she was still sitting at the edge of her bed, unmoving, as if transfixed by her own thoughts.

Accustomed to doing as she pleased, Beth pushed the door open, peeked in and spoke to her sister. "Wanna talk about it?"

Almost as immediately as the next second, Kate's eyes filled with tears. Seeing the glittering tears in her younger sister's eyes, Beth stepped inside of the pink, glowing bedroom and closed the door quietly. The older sister settled onto the floor carefully. She had never been as flexible or fit as her younger sister, and such motions took her more effort to complete.

"Tell me what happened," Beth probed.

"Oh nothing," Kate started, "Just I'm sure both Jim and Max think I'm some kind of racist coward."

Beth's eyes widened in alarm. "Where the heck did he take you?"

"We went to Max's coffee shop." Kate answered. Seeing Beth's nod, Kate continued. "We were just going to pop in for some coffee, but then Max came out and started talking to us."

"Well Max is cool," Beth assured.

Kate sat quietly, not answering or agreeing. Her sister waited patiently, believing that more would be shared, something critical to help her better understand why Kate was upset.

Kate blinked and felt the very warm tears race down her cheeks. Instead of responding directly, Kate asked, "Did you know that Max was one hundred percent Scottish? But also half Jewish? And that she has a thousand year old chicken noodle soup recipe?" Kate paused to hear a reply. Hearing none, she added, "Oh, and also that she's probably going to solve all the world's problems because she goes to political rallies?"

Beth squinted, trying to discern her sister's strange communication. In truth, she felt that Kate had always been this way. To Beth's thinking, Kate was like a pretty pair of shoes that you could never wear. Like a doll that you couldn't really play with. If you tried to play with the doll, if you tried to wear the shoes, they would simply break apart,--unable to bear the wear and tear of normal handling.

"Well, *whatever happened*, I'm sure it couldn't have been that bad," Beth falsely comforted, beginning to stand to her feet.

Out of nowhere, the two daughters could hear their parents laughing loudly. Their dad had turned on his favorite collection of Christmas songs. Various members of the Rat Pack were crooning expertly, as their parents danced awkwardly but passionately around their crowded living room.

"I'm gonna go hang out with Mom and Dad, and get some eggnog," Beth shared. "You comin'?"

Kate shook her head, then decided to speak, "Not right now."

Beth exited the room casually, closing the door behind her without looking back to see the distressed look on her sister's face.

Kate slammed her bedroom light switch to the off position, and struggled to situate herself comfortably in the bed. She hoped for complete darkness, having forgotten how much ambient light twinkled into her room now that practically all of the houses on the street were brightly lit by colorful, Christmas bulbs.

Kate settled into a loose fetal position. She'd had moments like this her whole life. Though she often meant well, she would say the wrong words, and misrepresent herself. The incidents left her feeling stupid, and completely misunderstood. She used the

edge of her pink bed sheet to wipe her tears. The material was soft and comforting. Despite having her family right in the very same house, Kate felt completely alone. She pressed her palm to her forehead, massaging her face to avoid getting a headache. Breathing deeply as she did so, she suddenly had a moment of clarity:
 She was attracted to the men she had dated because they always knew who they were. They spoke *clearly*. They stated their thoughts,--*their own opinions*--unapologetically. They *told* you if you were right. They *told* you if you were wrong. And it was all according to their strong, unwavering code of ethics. She felt safe with men like that. You knew what they expected out of you, and if you gave it to them, they were happy. *Usually*.

On a whim, Kate grabbed her cell phone. Before she let herself consider the ramifications, she scrolled through her contacts and sent a message to Derek, her *mostly* ex-boyfriend, just to see if he would respond. *"Let's have kids,"* her message read. She cradled the phone to her chest, quite compelled to see what he would say.

Waiting for a response, she fell asleep.

3 SLOUCH POTATO

Just a day later, things settled into a predictable, comforting Christmas rhythm.

The parents and the two sisters fell into the pleasant boredom that inevitably settles in during every Winter break. In an effort to entertain themselves, ancient board games were resurrected from the basement. A checkerboard with *almost enough pieces* was put into play. Old rivalries were re-ignited as the parents and their adult daughters bartered and coerced one another into lopsided, greedy *Monopoly* exchanges. Even the family's beautiful Backgammon board was brought upstairs for their enjoyment. However, as the family struggled once again to understand the rules of engagement, the immaculate game was shoved back into a darkened closet, and resigned out of play as usual.

As the hours passed, Kate was starting to feel better than she had in months. Something about the warm, almost lazy pace of the day had been healative. Her parents being close by,--and both of them being healthy, was a *huge blessing*, and she knew it. Though imperfect, her parents had always been well-meaning. Gentle. They had the sweet, natural balance that exists between a couple whose marriage had survived three decades. It was a harsh contrast to Kate and her beaus. Yet, thinking of Derek and the poor way things had ended, along with the rough and clumsy way that things had begun with Jim, Kate felt convinced that none of those things mattered. Nothing mattered but being home with her sister, her parents and her being able to take naps in her father's easy chair.

Beth had been over-indulging in eggnog, but no one complained. Kate watched as her sister laced her nog with more and more whisky each time she visited the kitchen. Kate preferred the holiday Sangria she had prepared. She had described the drink as "punch" to her mother, leaving out the fact that the drink was 90% wine. Her mother had enjoyed the "punch," quite a bit and had been laughing freely throughout the past few evenings. She also enjoyed how soundly the "punch" made her sleep. The peace could have gone on undisturbed, Kate supposed, for the rest of the holiday break, settled into the family nest amongst actual human beings. She'd spent *too* much time working from home over the past few months and was in *no* rush to return to her own empty, cold apartment.

Unfortunately, if there's anything that can be stated fairly about sisters, it's that they have a hard time leaving 'well-enough' alone. This was certainly true about Beth, *especially* as it related to Kate's love life. So perhaps it was Kate's fault that she was caught unawares by the sound of her parents' doorbell ringing loudly,--with a handsome man standing just outside of the doorway.

"Hey folks," Kate heard someone say. She now recognized Jim's voice immediately, though she *hoped* it was merely her imagination.

At the moment, Kate was slouching terribly, wearing one of her father's tired, oversized sweaters. It was a large, loose fitting cable knit sweater with a ripped collar,--a remnant from her father's heavier days. During her visits, Kate often snuggled into the huge garment like a hermit crab. Her father would have tossed it out long ago, but it was one of the few sweaters his wife had begun knitting and actually *completed*.

Kate glanced over her crumpled ensemble, she mused that her faded, green plaid pajama pants were *perfectly complemented* by her Sangria-stained house booties. Then, in a disturbingly familiar scene, Kate demanded of her sister, "What is *Jim* doing here?"

"I called him," Beth admitted, shrugging nonchalantly. "Look," she continued, "You never told me what happened. So I figured it couldn't have been that bad."

"Oh it's *that* bad," Kate refuted. "I'm surprised he even came. I told you he thinks I'm a raging maniac."

"Oh he does not," Beth insisted. "Besides, you're beautiful. If worst comes to worst, just flash him your tits and he'll forget whatever he was mad about."

With that sage advice, Beth moved away to welcome the man she hoped would one day be her brother in law, ignoring the sounds of objection Kate was making in the kitchen.

"Flash him your tits." Kate snarled, recalling the humiliating picture Derek had taken of her in Jamaica. "I have proof that's not how it works."

"She's right here," Kate heard Beth explain. And with that, both Beth and Jim were standing in the kitchen.

Kate, though dressed and covered from head to toe, felt naked as she stood in her parent's kitchen wearing dowdy, poorly fitting clothes and absolutely no make up.

"I wasn't expecting you," Kate admitted.

"Oh sure you were," Beth corrected. "He's come to get the gift you got for him."

"Yeah, and I brought you something, too,--something nice." Jim effused.

Kate's confusion was only temporary, as her sister's plot to have Jim return gained instant clarity. "So of course, *I* have a gift for *you*, too. Right?" she asked, turning her attention to Beth.

She watched as Beth nodded approvingly.

"Except I don't have a gift for you," Kate admitted, her voice flat with the truth.

"*Here!*" Beth falsely corrected. "Your gift isn't *here*. It must be over at Kate's apartment." Beth stared at Kate with bulging, pleading eyes.

Kate rolled her eyes and walked away. She shoved the door to the backyard open and stepped out.

Beth followed, smiling at Jim as she walked away.

"Kate," she rasped, stepping out onto the patio where her sister had ventured, "What the hell?!"

"What the hell, indeed," Kate countered. "You keep inviting that guy here like you're expecting some kind of magical Christmas romance to happen. And *nothing* is going to happen."

"What are you talking about? He *likes* you," Beth insisted.

"No, he doesn't," said Kate, looking her sister squarely in the eye. "And even if he does, *so what*?"

Beth stood still, surprised by her sister's objections.

"He seems like a nice guy. And yeah, he's kind of hot. But if you like him so much, why don't *you* date him?" Kate gibed.

Beth folded her arms in protest, "Oh, please." She took a moment to huff with irritation before continuing, "We were both standing there the night he brought the tree. The two of you locked eyes and that was it. I could have been standing there *naked* with a Rudolph the Reindeer red glowing nose, and he wouldn't have so much as noticed me."

Kate sighed and turned away.

"Look Kate, who was it that convinced you to try out for the dance team in your senior year?"

Kate shrugged, and admitted, "You."

"And who was it that told you how great you'd be as an account executive? Helped you get the job?"

Kate sighed. "You Beth."

"That's right," Beth boasted. "Because I know better than you. You have SO many opportunities, but you would just let them all pass you by. And if you're not careful, *Jim* is going to be one of those opportunities."

****

It was those words that were still rattling around her brain as she opened the door to her apartment.

Jim followed her inside, but stopped almost instantly.

"Wow, this place is clean."

"Yeah, he,--*we* had it decorated. *Professionally*." Kate boasted.

Jim nodded and stood awkwardly in the doorway. He regretted not having changed out of his work clothes. Thankfully, he'd spent the majority of that day working indoors, checking through the plumbing and HVAC system of a local university. All the same, he felt like he was covered with dust and grime as he observed Kate's upscale furnishings. The room looked like a page from a house decorating magazine.

"Come on in," Kate insisted. Moving to the kitchen, she offered, "I have wine, I have spritzer, I have beer. It's all ice cold. Been sitting in the fridge, forever."

Instead, Jim had instinctively grabbed Kate's tv remote and settled into the corner edge of the seat.

It was an action that Kate lamented almost immediately. She had recently ordered *"A Very Charlie Brown Christmas,"* and it was still on her screen when Jim switched on her set.

"I was gonna babysit," she lied, "And I thought the kids might like it."

"I love this movie," Jim blurted, not hearing Kate's unconvincing fib. "It's one of my faves."

"Oh yeah, it's okay I guess." Kate shrugged nonchalantly to better sell her false indifference.

"Wanna watch it?" Jim asked, though he was already cueing up the movie and removing his shoes.

Kate nodded then excused herself to the bathroom.

In truth, what she needed was a moment to find a halfway decent object to "re-gift." She disliked having to whip something together as a last minute gift for Jim. She doubted that the very thorough Derek had left behind anything of value. He had swept through on his last visit and cleaned house pretty well. He'd even taken the last half of a Cuban panini that had *technically* belonged to Kate.

Looking through drawers that she had once allowed Derek to call "his drawers," she found an untouched bottle of lotion that she had bought for him. She had bought the lotion while traipsing through the Galleria mall. She'd actually stopped in the store to find a new lotion or scent for herself. But as she browsed the shelves of the "men's section," she felt drawn in by the smooth dark glass bottles. Sniffing and smelling each one, Kate had selected a citrus and ylang ylang based lotion, then presented the heartfelt gift to Derek with genuine excitement.

"It's cute, babe." He had said, paying more attention to the receipt than to the actual item itself. "Didn't cost much, did it?" he inquired.

"Actually it did," she countered. "It was fifteen dollars."

Derek had laughed heartily at Kate's comment, thinking she was making an actual joke. Reading his reaction, Kate had joined into the laughter. The two had gone back to watching tv soon after. She had never seen Derek use the lotion. Had never smelled it on him. Now, looking through his drawers, she saw that the bottle had been left behind, its plastic seal unbroken. Kate picked up the gift and considered giving it to Jim. But for reasons she couldn't explain, she couldn't bring herself to do so. She took a breath and braced herself to tell her guest the truth and apologize for not providing him with a gift.

But instead of waiting expectantly for his present, Jim was thoroughly enjoying himself, smiling and totally engrossed in the beginning scenes of his favorite Peanut's cartoon.
When he caught sight of Kate, he stopped the film and began to scroll back. "Sorry," he grinned. "I'll restart it."

"No, it's fine," she said. "I'm used to it. My boyfriend Derek would watch movies all the time. If I wasn't ready for the movie to start, he would just tell me to watch it again later. He *hated* rewatching scenes." Kate snorted, enjoying her own short story.

"You have a boyfriend?" Jim probed.

Kate realized her mistake, but felt oddly calm as she corrected herself. "Actually no," she admitted. "I have an ex-boyfriend. We never officially broke up, but he hasn't called me for like, *months*." She felt a little emotional as she admitted the truth, felt an achy sting at the back of her throat.

Jim probed a bit further. "So it wasn't really serious or anything?"

"Oh no, it was," Kate corrected. "That's part of what made it so weird. We were dating. We were serious. We never really talked about marriage, so much. But you know, we talked about how life would be if we ever had kids. Or like," Kate swallowed and looked upward to keep from crying and to keep control of her voice, "what life would be like for the *two of us* once the pandemic was over."

Jim noticed the glaze of fresh tears in Kate's blue eyes. She seemed to cry easily, he noticed. It was a trait he found sweet about most girls. Besides, talking about her boyfriend was probably hard for her, he reasoned. So Jim felt somewhat glad to be there for her, available to listen. It had actually been a long time since he'd been able to simply sit and listen to a beautiful woman express her feelings. He spent most of his days locked in his office reading through complicated proposals, reviewing building plans, or stomping through muddy construction sites, arguing with bull-headed site workers who didn't want to do their job,--*or who complained to Jim that he didn't know how to do his own.* His work was demanding, often consisting of more fast paced special projects than the slower, bulk work of traditional construction jobs. It didn't leave much time for dating.

So it was very nice to sit next to Kate, a pretty person with a small, delicate chin, who was waving her small, dainty hands in exasperated expression as she unloaded her feelings upon him. *Trusting me,* he thought. *She's trusting me with her feelings.* He noticed that Kate stopped speaking suddenly and was looking downward at her hands, now cupped together and resting in her lap.

"I'm sorry," she whined softly, demurely. "I'm sure you didn't want to hear all that. I know guys don't like when girls talk too much, especially about other guys."

Jim paused the movie and sat up at attention. "No, no. It doesn't bother me at all. I'm glad you were telling me about,--what was his name?"

Kate chuckled a tiny bit. "Derek. My sister Beth calls him 'Derek the butthole.' "

Jim laughed. "That's the lady with the darker hair, kind of wavy? I figured she was your sister. You guys favor a little. She's a bit heavier than you. Her voice is a little raspier."

Kate felt minorly offended at Jim's ungracious description of her sister. "Well she's a teacher," Kate defended. "She hardly ever gets out to exercise. And her voice has gotten raspier over the years because she just does SO much talking." Kate paused long enough to search out Jim's eyes. "I mean have you been inside of a classroom lately? The kids are freaking *nuts.*"

"No, I know," Jim agreed. "I wasn't saying all that stuff in a bad way. I just meant..." Jim's voice trailed off as he searched for words. Thinking of none that could redeem his previous statement, he decided a distraction tactic might work better. "So who's really been calling my office? Has that been you? Or Beth? The person leaving the message has been leaving your name, but the voice sounds more *raspy.*"

Kate blushed a bit, immediately forgetting her offense at Jim's previous statement. Searching for words, she blinked her eyes repeatedly and smiled nervously.

Jim smiled warmly, feeling that he had a genuine grasp of the situation. "So it's your sister that's been calling, saying that it's you. But really, it's been her the whole time."

Kate's eyes closed slowly, dramatically. "Yes," she said softly. Her eyes opened quickly because she could feel a slight brush of breath across her face. Jim had leaned in closely, more closely than she was accustomed to these days. *Breath. Sighs. Hands.* These things that had once been so harmless, *so common*, now put her on edge. Every stranger's breath had to be viewed like a weapon, almost like toxic waste. Now, instead of six feet of social distance, Jim's face was barely six inches away from her own.

"Well," he moaned softly, "I think it's really, really sweet." His eyes roamed over her face, his warm gaze just barely glazing over the skin of her neck. He refused his eyes the pleasure of searching over the curves of her breasts. Instead, he forced his eyes back upward to her own. "You know," he started, his breath once again grazing her lips and chin, "I think we had it right when we said 'baby blue' for your eyes. That's the right color. Definitely baby blue."

Kate smiled, noticeably charmed by his words. She had forgotten that part of their conversation at the cafe. Her mind had only ever replayed her conversation with Max. She could still see Max's crimson colored locks swimming about her face and shoulders. Still remembered the seductive way Max's young body had moved beneath her sexy crop top. The small, alluring belly ring.

Before she knew it, Jim's hands were cupping her face, causing Kate's heart to pound instantly. Jim's gaze was intentful, earnest, thought not lustful, she noted. At the same time, his touch was still strange to her skin. She didn't know him that well. And with things being so weird, so...dangerous. It was hard to simply be "caught up in the moment."

Jim's voice broke into her reverie, "Can I kiss you, Kate?" he asked politely. His amber colored eyes were warm again, the way they had been the first night they met. Warm, bright, sweet brown eyes.

"I don't know." She said. "Are you sick? And like, have you *been* sick? Or showing symptoms within the last 20 days?"

Unoffended, Jim shook his head, 'no.'

"What about friends and family," she continued. "Is anyone in your house sick? Friends? Coworkers?"

Kate's impromptu interrogation caused a sudden bubble of laughter to erupt inside of her handsome new friend. He leaned back and quietly laughed at her words. Nothing she had asked was remotely romantic. And he wondered if the seductive moment was lost. All the same, he thought she was smart for taking precautions. He was glad to see that she wasn't silly or frivolous about such things.

Jim's soft laughter caused Kate to relax and she joined into his amusement, chuckling a bit at her behaviour, and the entire situation.

"I'm sorry," she pleaded. "It's just that,--"

"It's just that you have to be careful. We have to take precautions. You're *right*," Jim finished. "And you asking those questions tells me that you're smart, too. Not just beautiful."

Kate's eyes opened widely at the compliment. "Thank you." She cooed.

Jim leaned in again, feeling the heat of connection once again warm the room. His pointer finger touched the tip of Kate's knee as his eyes traveled upward to her mouth.

"*But*," he emphasized, "you never really answered my question." Jim brushed gossamer hairs back from the edges of Kate's delicate cheekbones. "Can I kiss you?"

Kate's pulse picked up in intensity again, thrumming in her throat and wrists.

Her mouth opened to respond, but she found Jim's soft lips falling atop her own. The very heat from his skin was so erotic, so pleasurable. It was surprising how quickly a male's presence could begin to feel strange. Thrilling, but unnerving. She thought it would be nice to simply have him hold her close. Kiss her lips, make her feel safe.

"Wait," she said, putting her hand to Jim's surprisingly firm, muscled chest. Kate forced herself to think clearly. "I've never been a tease. Like, I don't lead guys on. So you can kiss me," she offered, her voice barely above a whisper. "But that's really *it*, okay?"

The corner of Jim's mouth pulled into a gentle smile. He took a second to breathe deeply, simply enjoying the very smell of Kate's warm, clean scent. It was obvious that she was a nice girl, he thought. And you didn't rush nice girls. You wanted to, because, well, nature just has a way of making a man's blood run fire hot when a beautiful woman was close to him. But he had no intention of making her do what she didn't want to do, wasn't *ready* to do.

Jim, lifted Kate's hand and caressed it with the gentlest of kisses. After honoring her fingers with the delicate touches of his mouth, he gazed into her eyes again and replied, "I think for tonight, kissing you is more than enough."

Kate nibbled the edge of her lip, and looking into the gentleman's eyes, she nodded in agreement. The gesture encouraged Jim to lean in closely. His kiss was now stronger than before, more firm, though not overwhelming. Her hand found the collar of his shirt, and her fingers gently stroked the edge of this strong, elegantly muscled neck.

Jim's lips moved tenderly and hungrily across Kate's mouth for only a few moments. Showing great restraint, he pulled away and opened his eyes.

Kate's eyes opened more slowly than his own, and she was surprised to see him starting so intently at her. His gaze was unflinching, but not critical. Those amber eyes seemed to be gently appreciating her, sipping in her sweetness and beauty. Still, the moments after a kiss had always made Kate feel oddly awkward. Without meaning to, she blurted, "Do you *really* like "A Charlie Brown Christmas?"

The corner's of Jim's eyes curled in delighted amusement. He answered sincerely, "It's my favorite."

The next day found Kate strolling about a local mall, searching for a nice gift for Jim. They had been texting off and on all day, and Kate couldn't help but feel lighter than air as his texts became sweeter and more romantic with each passing hour.

It's funny how a new romance changes one's outlook on life. Just a few days before, Christmas had felt empty. The bright lights and cheery music had seemed artificial and hollow. But with a new beau texting her sweet nothings, the holiday seemed hopeful again, full of good will. Just as she was about to enter into a shop, her phone rang. Hoping it was Jim, she answered quickly, "Hey you…"

"Hey. Stop and get eggs," Beth replied, flatly.

"Oh crap, I thought you were Jim." Kate answered. Her statement triggered her sister's intense curiosity.

Beth crooned, "Oh really?" She chuckled softly. "And please don't think I missed the fact that you did *not* come back to Mom and Dad's last night."

"I was busy," Kate defended.

"You were with *Jim*," Beth insisted. "So," she continued, "I'm assuming he took you into his arms and made mad passionate love to you all night?"

"No way," Beth objected. "I mean, I just met him. And he's handsome and all, and very sweet, but…" Kate's voice trailed off. She hadn't meant to stop speaking, but her thoughts were eloping to the night before. Jim really had been such a darling. Before she knew it, the two of them had been snuggled together on her sofa. Jim had been telling the truth about his fondness of the cartoon. His familiarity with the movie had become obvious as he'd acted out his favorite lines throughout the cartoon. Kate had found the whole scene hilarious. After several minutes into the movie,

Kate stepped away quietly. Remembering that she was the hostess, she decided to make a snack.

"Making popcorn for us?"

Kate spun around, surprised to see that Jim had padded into the kitchen behind her, not unlike a hungry puppy.

"Well I wasn't sure what I would make," she admitted, as she browsed through her somewhat sparse offerings. She hadn't been grocery shopping recently, with the threat of the virus still hanging in the air.

"If you have regular kernels, I know how to pop them," Jim announced, obviously proud of his culinary prowess, however meager.

"A-ha!" Kate shouted as she eyed a box of microwave popcorn. Upon opening the box, she pulled out its contents and showed them to Jim. "Just one pack left. You," she said, pointing her finger at his muscled chest, "are a lucky boy."

Moved by a wave of desire, Jim gently scooped Kate into his arms. "You are so sweet and cute," he told her, his mouth moving closer. "I really like you Kate."

Feeling warmed by his presence, Kate allowed herself to relax in his embrace. Her eyes spied his strong, thick forearms. Her fingers traced upward on his arm.

"I like you, too," she admitted.
Jim smiled and watched her expression for clues as he asked, "So, are you available? You're not really seeing anybody right now are you?"

Kate shrugged, suddenly shy about the truth of being single. She wasn't playing hard to get, but didn't know exactly what words to say. She didn't want to move too fast. This man, however gorgeous, was still something of a stranger to her.

"Well," Jim started, as if reading her thoughts. "I'm not really involved with anyone, either. I've got a good paying job. Never been to jail."

Kate laughed loudly, nervously, "Well that's good to know."

Smiling, Jim continued, "I like long walks on the beach, drinking wine as I watch the sunset."

"Naturally," Kate interrupted, amused by his cliches, which seemed borrowed from vintage personal ads. "And of course, you love children. And puppies!"
"Love 'em!" Jim said, giving Kate's body a small reassuring squeeze.

Kate's eyes searched Jim's face. It was strange how comfortable she felt in his embrace. She felt safer, more herself and more at ease with Jim than she had *ever* felt with Derek,--even after months of dating. Derek had often seemed on the edge of snapping at her. Was always somewhat disapproving. Truthfully, she felt she had grown as a person with Derek. He was the one who had bought the furniture for her apartment. They had tossed out the furniture left over from her college days: her futon with the dingy plaid cushions and the ripped seam. Her pictures of cute animals she had placed in plastic, dollar store frames. Her comfortable corduroy chair, *a gift she had inherited from her beloved grandfather*. Deliveries from upscale shops had swiftly elevated her loft from cheap to chic. Cool. "Cold really," she had thought, once the apartment was completed. But she hadn't dared to object.

Kate's eyes found the rounded, muscular form of Jim's right shoulder. She inquired softly, "So, let's say it's Christmas day. Where would you rather be? At home, in your junky old grandparent's house, or somewhere kind of hot and tropical, like Jamaica?"

Jim barely blinked before answering, "Well, Jamaica. Christmas is always so cold." Thinking for only a second longer, he added, "But only if my whole family could go. Otherwise, I guess, just hanging out at my grandparents house. Better to be with family, freezing my butt off than hanging out on some beach by myself." Jim released Kate as he further considered the truth. He picked up the pack of popcorn Kate had found and began to unwrap the snack.

"Especially now," he continued. "My grandfather has gotten to be a bit of a handful. We think he's got dementia, but he won't go to the doctor. Grandma needs all the help she can get."

Jim popped the popcorn into the microwave and slid easily onto one of Kate's small metal counter stools. "What about you?" Jim asked. "Jamaica or junky old house?"

Kate smiled, "Junky old house. With grandparents. Aunts and uncles. Just, anywhere my family is," she informed him.

Jim smiled warmly, "Nice."

✶✶✶✶✶✶✶✶✶✶✶✶✶✶✶✶✶✶✶✶✶✶

Beth's voice interrupted Kate's extended reverie. "He's sweet but what?"

Kate felt confused, having lost track of her own thoughts ages ago. She realized that she had wandered into a boutique and was standing next to a display of colognes.

"Do you think Jim would like cologne?" Kate asked her sister, who had gone silent.

"Just don't forget the eggs, Dum-dum." Beth answered.

The call ended.

4
SHUT THE TYKE UP

With a new gift in hand, Kate swung out of the mall parking lot feeling light, but accomplished. It really was nice to have her job as an account executive. The marketing agency she worked for always took an extended break over the holidays. The money was great. It was yet another opportunity her sister Beth had coordinated for her.

 With the onset of the pandemic, there were moments when Beth wished she'd had the courage to take the account executive position for herself. She had grown tired of school district politics and endlessly shifting protocols. Teaching had shifted from being an endless, exhausting adventure to being a hellish, frightening nightmare. As parents in her district put pressure on the district and demanded in-person instruction, Beth found herself feeling increasing nervous and fearful. She had been called a coward to her face. Everyone seemed so unhinged and triggered.

Though the opportunity had presented itself over a year ago, Beth remembered her friends enticing words.

"The pay is pretty good," Dana had said. "Plus you'd be able to have a freaking life,--finally," Dana jibed.

Beth had continued to listen, watching the employees shift in and out of the building. To Beth, they all seemed so young and stylish. And *slim*. Beth had taken a quick glance in the rearview mirror. To her own eyes, she'd looked tired. Overweight. And older than her age of 29 would indicate. Her eyes were as blue as her sister Kate's, though her hair was much darker, nose a bit wider, cheeks quite a bit rounder.

Dana had only rolled her eyes again as she watched her friend make faces in the rearview mirror before pulling off into traffic. "Anyway, think about it."

Beth had thought about it, and decided it was a great opportunity. *For Kate.* She'd fit right in with all of the pretty people floating in and out of the building. Plus the kid would finally have a real job with real benefits. She respected Kate's working in an animal shelter, but in Beth's opinion, her younger sister was letting her freshly earned degree go to waste.

****

Tucked safely in her parent's garage, Kate grabbed Jim's gift. She couldn't resist giving it another sniff. The scent was rich, luscious with hints of cardamom, pepper and cypress. She couldn't wait to smell it on Jim. The night he had dropped by he'd smelled a bit-workman like. It hadn't bothered her. Derek had always smelled expensive cologne, though she had never liked the scent.

Derek had called it a *"statement scent, not one you have to like."* To Kate's mind, he wore too much of it, as if *insisting* that people ask him what cologne he was wearing. Remembering Derek irritated Kate increasingly, and she couldn't help but roll her eyes She hopped out of the car and settled into the warmth of the family's kitchen.

Hours later, Kate found herself being gently awakened by a buzzing sensation near her waist. Sleepily, her hands searched to find her phone. The buzzing ended before she found it. So, hoping the call was unimportant, she allowed herself to drift off to sleep again.

Seconds later, the buzzing resumed.

"Good grief," she grumbled sleepily, but her eyes were now fully open. She'd missed the call again, but reasoned that the call must be the same person. Checking her call logs, she saw that she had missed four calls, all within a half hour.

"That's Jim," she thought, cheerfully. After calling him back, Jim answered instantly.

His voice was bright with excitement. "Hey!" he shouted. "Sorry about all the phone calls. I need to ask you a favor."

Two hours later, and five outfits later, Kate found herself standing on the porch of Jim's parents' home. It was an expansive ranch, with perfectly manicured boxwoods that had been expertly draped with white lights. She had barely touched the doorbell when Jim spilled out unto the porch, snatching the door closed behind him.

"Okay, just about everybody in my entire family is here tonight." He said tensely, "Even more people than I expected."

Kate nodded her head but felt confused, "Is that a good thing, or a problem or what?"

Jim explained, "I don't know, it's just a bit weird." Taking Kate by the arm he pulled her away from the doorway. "I mean, since we just met, I wasn't really planning to invite you over, honestly. Didn't want you to feel pressured or anything. But then *Bigmouth*," Jim continued, referring to his younger brother, "Bigmouth decides to mention to my parents that I'd started seeing someone. And my mother..." Jim's voice trailed off as he looked upward, as if soliciting help from the heavens.

Kate chuckled silently, "Say no more. I get it." She smiled and touched a button on Jim's well worn plaid shirt. "Tell you what, expect me to be the perfect, new girlfriend tonight. I'll smile. Shake hands. Sit and look pretty."

"Well you can do more than that," Jim started, but he was soon interrupted by the sound of the front door opening. Jim pulled Kate toward him to evade peeping eyes. His name was being bellowed by a curious aunt who'd noticed he had gone missing.

"Well," Jim started, resignedly, "Let's see how this goes."

Following behind him eagerly, Kate took careful, delicate steps into the house. She was glad she had worn her smoky brick red lipstick. It matched the red of Jim's shirt perfectly. She had already figured out that Jim didn't notice or care about such things. But to Kate, sweet little things like that mattered.

Her introduction to Jim's mother had gone well, Kate felt. Jack Townsley, Jim's father had done Kate the favor of introducing her as "the daughter of one of his best customers." That seemed to please Jim's mother, who smiled and shook Kate's hand.

"Well, I'm Patricia. Just call me Trish." Then feeling the warmth of the Christmas spirits she had been imbibing all night, Trish leaned in and gave Kate a small hug before hollering out, "Happy Christmas!"

Jim had made a brief, quiet, general introduction of Kate, before stepping away to hang up her coat. Kate found herself suddenly surrounded by many sets of curious eyes, both young and old. Kate smiled and shook hands easily, taking the time to gently cup the hands of each aunt as she was introduced. As Kate was ushered around the home, she took a moment to touch the bangs of one particularly blonde little girl and called her "adorable," a gesture which seemed to instantly charm the child's mother, one of Jim's older cousins. Kate spied an extremely old couple sitting together in the corner of the great room, near the fireplace. The wife appeared to be settling her husband with a blanket. Kate thought the old woman looked tired, but peaceful. The elderly man looked slightly confused, but allowed himself to be tucked in the well-meaning "old woman" who was caring for him.

"Aww, Jim's grandparents," Kate thought.

With the exception of the older couple sitting peacefully in the great room, Jim's entire family seemed vibrant and energetic. They had been very warm and friendly, making Kate feel instantly at home.

One uncle in particular seemed to love being the center of attention. He told jokes for minutes on end. Some of them were even funny, though most were not. All the same, he had called Kate 'absolutely lovely,' upon meeting her, so she was happy to smile and laugh politely at his jokes.

Jim had looked strangely tense the entire evening. He had downed at least three shots of something, plus two beers. It didn't unnerve Kate. She was used to guys getting themselves sauced. Besides, she had only had a small glass of hard mulled cider and was planning to drive herself home at the end of the evening, no designated driver required.

Kate had just sipped her drink and politely refused a glass of spiked eggnog when an odd hush befell the room. As voices went silent, the sound of a television playing *"The Sound of Music"* became very audible.

"That's one of my favorite musicals," Kate said, her voice suddenly seeming too loud and cheerful for the room.

"Is that right?" Kate heard someone ask, the voice dripping with oily sarcasm. She turned to see a fit-bodied man, heavily tatted man standing next to a crock pot. The man looked around for a spoon for about half of a second, before deciding to simply dip his finger into the pot of warm cheese dip.

"Put on a shirt, Tyke" Kate heard Trish complain to the tattooed man,--Jim's younger brother. The young man barely acknowledged his mother's words. Kate knew it was highly unlikely that he would put on a shirt, as requested. Not someone tattooed as him. All the guys she knew who had tats were *super* proud of them and very eager to show them off, *constantly*.

"Nice ink," Kate said, adding a little edge, and taking some of the cheer out of her voice. "What's that like, 60% body coverage?"

"More like 70," Tyke corrected sharply. "But I don't know, because I don't get ink to compete with others."

"Oh no, I know it's not a competition," Kate insisted, her hands held up in a defensive position, a subconscious gesture meant to convey benevolence.

Tyke tossed a couple of nuts into his mouth and searched over Kate's body with his eyes, assessing her openly. He nodded. "Alright. Let's see your ink."

Kate laughed nervously, "Oh I don't have any. Never had the guts."

A nearby aunt chuckled, but agreed, "Me either, babe. I thought I'd try one day, but--"

"So you're a coward," Tyke cut in, his eyes stabbing into Kate. "And a hypocrite. The kind of person who's all like, 'Oh, I like your tats,'" he continued, imitating a syrupy, sing-song voice as he did so, "meanwhile, what you're actually thinking is that you're too good to let somebody put an actual tat on you."

Kate shook her head profusely, "No not at all. I was just saying that I kind of think it's cool, is all."

Tyke hissed and rolled his eyes. "Okay well, ink is not meant to be cool, okay? It's a lifestyle. It's who I am."

"It's a compliment," Kate heard a man say suddenly, the voice booming into the kitchen with somewhat angry authority. Kate turned and was glad to see Jim re-entering the room. "Just take it as a compliment," Jim finished, his voice settling into a slightly less authoritative tone.

"I didn't say it wasn't a compliment," Tyke defended. But Kate noticed how the younger man suddenly seemed smaller, less impressive, despite the aggressively themed tattoos that laced his naked upper body.

Jim moved closer to Kate, though he didn't turn to face her.

"Where've you been?" Kate whispered, semi-playfully.

Jim's face remained unsmiling as he leaned closer to his date and whispered, "Sitting with my grandparents. You seemed to be doing alright when I left," he told her. Then turning to face her, he added, "But just be careful with what you say tonight, okay?"

The mood lightened soon however, as one of Jim's aunts reached into the fridge and pulled out a heavily decorated, beautiful chocolate cake. Fudgy fleur de lis bedecked the round chocolate beast, which had to be at least twelve inches wide, and several inches high. As the cake was placed upon the round kitchen table, a large flock of children instantly appeared in the kitchen. Jim used the moment to duck away and check on his grandfather, whom he could hear moaning.

One of the children pointed to the behemoth cake, allowing his finger to come dangerously close to the edge of the icing. "It's for Jesus' birthday," the child announced.

Kate evaded the religious comment smoothly, gesturing to the kids and saying sweetly, "They're all so cute."

Several of the women smiled and nodded, agreeing with Kate,and liking her even better for having appreciated the awesomeness of their children.

Unfortunately, Kate's words also caught Tyke's attention. Not missing a beat, he inquired. "You got kids?"

Though posed impolitely, Kate could see that the fellow women in the room seemed interested in her answer, despite themselves.

"No," Kate stated emphatically. "I don't have any kids."

"You don't like 'em?" Tyke asked. "It's alright with me if you don't. *I* don't really like 'em."

Kate sighed in slight exasperation despite herself, "No, it's not that I don't like kids. I *love* kids. It's just that I haven't had any yet."

Tyke smiled, and playfully tossed more nuts in his mouth. "So you like kids, but you don't have any. You like tats, but you don't have any." He chuckled. "Let me guess, you're waiting for Mr. Right to come along and tell you when you're *supposed* to settle down, and when you're *supposed* to start making babies. Right?"

Kate looked at her boots and didn't reply.

Tyke continued, "Meanwhile, you've got to keep that skin of yours lily white and perfect, right? Why?" He leaned in close to Kate, but said loudly for everyone to hear, "...So nobody gets a real clue as to how much mileage you're *actually* putting on that ass."

"That's enough, Tyke," Trish cut in, the drink in her hand splashing on her fingers. Then, turning to Kate, she said, "Don't pay any attention. He's just always been this way. Always been so mean."

Kate shrugged and nodded casually. In truth, she felt deeply insulted by Tyke's words. His accusations had hit a nerve, though she was unsure as to why. Feeling the urge to step away from the others, her feet started traveling out of the kitchen toward the family's spacious, white dining room.

"Trust me," Trish slurred, clumsily following Kate as she moved away. Unbeknownst to Trish, Tyke followed the two women as well, sensing the need to hear his mother's next remark.

Trish leaned toward Kate and attempted to speak in a quiet voice. Her words were emboldened by her drinks as she expressed her honest feelings, "You picked the good one, Kate. Jim? He's the *good* one."

Insulted by his mother's words, Tyke's eyes glazed over with icy fire. Then without looking in Jim's direction, Tyke spoke loudly enough for his brother and the rest of the family to hear his next words. "I dunno, Bro. This one's kind of boring. Besides, I thought you liked redheads now?"

"Just cool it," Jim warned, his voice tight with irritation. Then stepping closer to his brother, Jim narrowed his eyes and added, "I swear I'm gonna kick your ass."

Kate smiled despite herself. She wasn't sure if she was smiling because of Jim's coming to her defense, or because she believed what Trish had said, that Jim was *"the good one."* But one thing she did agree with for sure was that Tyke was mean.

Tyke turned to one of the small boy cousins who was sitting in the living room. "Go get me a beer," he ordered. "A cold one. *Quick.*"

"I think you ought to apologize," Jim informed his younger brother. "Kate's nice. And you've been insulting her all night."

Tyke stared at his brother, wide-eyed, wordless. When the boy returned with the beverage, Tyke held up the beer and shoved it toward Kate.

"Here you go. Drink this beer," he commanded. "It's my favorite kind. *Imported.*"

Kate sighed imperceptibly. She didn't care for beer, but she opened the bottle with the edge of her sleeve and took a swig obligingly.

"Great. Now let's go to the kitchen and have some cake," Tyke insisted.

Hearing Tyke's words and seeing that the young adults were heading back into the kitchen, the aunts busied themselves with handing out paper plates.

As a large slice of cake was handed to Kate, she considered the enormous amount of calories she would be ingesting. But Tyke's gaze was fixed on her intently. Wanting to appear fearless, Kate broke off a piece of cake with her fingers and shoved it into her mouth.

Tyke took a swig from the beer Kate had previously been drinking from. He hated seeing good beer go to waste. And as he swallowed the golden beverage, he knew that he also hated Kate.

"How's the cake?" he asked her.

Kate nodded and gave a thumbs up, charming the aunts who laughed heartily at her gesture of approval. In truth, Kate had barely tasted the cake. Her mind was occupied with thoughts of how to bring the evening to a pleasant enough close. She has promised Jim that she would be the *perfect new girlfriend*. Now here she was clashing with his brother terribly. Tyke seemed immune to her charms. Even though she knew it was Tyke who was being the disagreeable one, she couldn't help but feel that she was somehow failing Jim.

Tyke shoved Kate's beer back in her direction. "Take another swig."

Obliging him one last time, Kate tossed back the beer and forced down a swallow. She took another bite of cake just to drown out the flavor of the malt beverage. Jim watched as she seemed to cringe at the flavor of his favorite beer.

"D'you like the beer?" Tyke asked, his voice accusational and tense.

Kate smiled as she wiped fudge icing from her fingers. "Well, not really." She admitted.

Tyke smiled, somewhat broadly. Looked to Jim, then back at Kate. "You sat here drinking this beer, but you don't even like it. I can tell just by *looking* at you that you probably never eat cake, but you did it anyway." Tyke swore under his breath. "You're a slutty blonde idiot."

"Shut your big mouth," Jim commanded. "And apologize now."

"I'm doing *you* a favor," Tyke yelled, the angry tension in his voice causing the family to once again turn their attention in his direction.

Tyke leaned toward his brother, posturing himself defiantly as he spoke to his older sibling. "'Cause I swear, without my help, *you're* gonna end up marrying some brainless scoop of vanilla ice cream. One who doesn't know what she wants. Doesn't know who she is. And doesn't add a damn thing to you or this family."

Without hesitating, Kate defended, "I am not brainless." The anger in her own voice surprised her, but she was glad to have spoken up. "I know things," she finished, vaguely.

Tyke's eyebrow raised, "Okay great," he started. "Enlighten us. Why don't you tell us how you felt about, say, a proposition. Or an amendment,-- anything that was on the last ballot."

"Tyke's *political.*" From the corner, Trish's voice emerged loudly, though in stature she seemed shrunken, collapsed. "Whole family is, really," she admitted, chuckling into the ice of her mostly empty drink. "Too political."

Kate's brain remained froze at Tyke's question. For a moment she flashed back to the awkward moment in the cafe when she and Jim had been chatting with the vibrant and politically active shop owner, Maxine. Kate nibbled her lip and tried to remember something she had overhead Derek say about the state budget. And hadn't there been something about unions? Her brain was refusing to work. She shook her head and looked at her boots.

"It's alright," Tyke said, his words offering false reassurance. "Lots of people get confused about basic politics." He reached over to pull a piece of cake from Kate's plate. "So why don't you just teach us something else."

"What else?" Kate shot out, beginning to feel humiliated and angry.

"Anything else!" Tyke shot back.

"Be more specific," Kate returned, not feeling brave so much as she felt cornered, and duly aggressive.

"Tell us what you believe in. Tell us something you believe is worth dying for. Hell, tell us who you voted for!" Tyke demanded.

"I didn't vote!" Kate shouted in return.

Tyke's eyebrow raised as he let the effect of Kate's confession settle in around the table. He chortled. "Well, he said. "Not much of a surprise there."

Kate glanced around the room at Jim's family. Having just met them, she didn't know,--*couldn't* know that the family was passionately patriotic. They held deep-seated beliefs about voting and every person's "civic duty to their community." But she saw their faces, some of which looked embarrassed, some disapproving.

Speaking more than thinking, Kate continued to explain herself. "I just knew it wouldn't matter. It doesn't matter how you vote. Or what you think. *It doesn't matter*. Everything's decided before you get there." Kate shook her head as she confessed her feelings, her fears. She could feel her eyes filling with fresh tears as she saw how her words caused a couple of Jim's older relatives to stare at the floor uncomfortably.

Jim reached over to stroke Kate's back reassuringly. "I'll get your coat."

5

Can I Pour You Something to Think?

And just like that, it was Christmas.

Julia was all atwitter in the kitchen. She felt she had done a great job of hiding the girls' presents this year. She had hoped and prayed they would enjoy their presents as she placed them under the large, bedecked tree in their living room.

Beth was in unusually good spirits herself. She hadn't had a spot of drink this early a.m. But she had been buzzing and humming along with the lovely, bright feelings of the holiday coursing through her veins.

"Mom, I think the ham's ready!" she called out, trying to speak loudly enough to alert her mother without actually waking her younger sister.

Beth had heard Kate come in the night before. Her mood upon returning had been much darker than when she had left earlier that evening. Dressed in charcoal gray sateen pants, velvet blouse and a black leather peacoat, Beth had thought that Kate looked like a supermodel. It was always odd to her when things didn't go well for Kate. She saw in her sister *everything* a person needed to succeed: beauty, charm, a decent amount of brains. *Why did she have such a hard time with guys*? Gently, quietly, Beth had crept up the steps. It was only a half hour past 9 pm, and Kate had already tucked herself into bed. Beth listened for a while at the door. Though the tears were quiet, Beth could detect the muffled sounds of Kate's sobbing. Beth peeked into her sister's room. Kate hadn't even bothered to remove her boots before collapsing in bed. Beth stepped into the bedroom.

Kate, hearing someone enter, tried to stifle her tears. "I'm okay, I just need a minute," she choked out.

"You're fine," Beth said quietly. Then, moving toward the edge of the bed, she took hold of Kate's shoes, unzipped them gently, and removed each one. She pulled Kate's comforter from beneath her legs and spread it carefully. Beth moved toward the door, closed it softly behind her, and took a couple of steps down the staircase. Then, feeling deeply compelled to give greater care, she stepped back into Kate's room.

Kate felt the edge of her comforter being lifted, and felt her older sister settle in behind her, spooning Kate gently. Beth rested her face atop her sister's head

"You know what?" Beth began, speaking quietly, "You're good. You're a good person. And you're good enough." Hearing her words, Kate's body began to shake with heartfelt sobs. She closed her eyes and allowed her heart to drink in her sister's reassurances.

"I don't know what happened," Beth continued, "But I just know you're awesome." Beth swallowed. "And I give you a hard time sometimes, but you're a great kid and I'm super proud of you." In a surprise to herself, Beth's words weren't just affecting her sister. They were choking her up as well.

Kate's hand reached up and gently gripped her older sister's fingers. Beth squeezed Kate's hand in return before finishing, "And you know what? I'm always gonna look after you. I'm always gonna be here. *Screw guys*. We have each other, and that's what matters." Beth's eyes closed as she felt her own warm tears coursing down her cheeks. "We're both fine," she whispered. "We're gonna be fine." Kate had cried herself to sleep, and Beth herself had drifted off for an hour. Waking later, she'd said a short, simple prayer for her sister, then closed the door quietly behind her.

Kate had slept peacefully through the night.

****

Now, this fresh, bright Christmas morning, things were much more normal than anyone in the house had expected. With the pandemic rules still in effect, carollers weren't likely to grace their doorstep. Regardless, her father was happy to keep broadcasting cheerful holiday tunes throughout the house via his 50" television, complete with his new gift: a powerful subwoofer for his beloved television.

Kate moved herself to the bathroom. She felt a bit drained still, but not exhausted. Feeling unhurried, Kate took a few moments to indulge in some minor spa care. She let the water run until it was perfectly warm, then gently splashed her face with great, scooping handfuls of water. Enjoying the feel of the water, she decided to indulge in a full shower, complete with the expensive shower gel tucked away in her overnight bag. When Derek had given it to her, she had been afraid to use it. She knew it was expensive, which somehow seemed to make the shower gel "too good to use." Kate rolled her eyes at her own silliness. She borrowed a dab of her mother's face mask and spread it carefully. She thought to rinse it off, but decided to leave it on. She enjoyed seeing the gray paste on her face.

Preferring to be comfortable today, she put on a pair of striped fuzzy socks, tightened the belt of her pink, fleece robe and strolled down the stairs.

Unlike previous years, her mother had decided to slice and place all the foods on a large wooden platter, foregoing their traditional family dinner.

"It's a charcuterie!" Her mother had announced, hoping to delight her family with her trendy surprise. "It's been all the rage this year."

Beth and Kate enjoyed it greatly. Only their father had complained a bit. He had been hoping to have his wife's traditional foods, his beloved mac n cheese, and her delicious brown gravy of her somewhat lumpy mashed potatoes.

"Gotta be flexible," Kate had reminded her father. "Things don't always just go so perfectly. Gotta try new things." Kate wasn't sure if it was herself talking, or the large glass of spiced Sangria she was having at 11 am.

Her father had grumbled and whined while Kate slipped into the living room. Filled with meat, wine and cheeses, the pretty young woman took the moment to steal her father's unattended recliner, and drifted, to her surprise, right off to sleep.

****

"Hey," she heard as her eyes were fluttering back open.

To Kate's surprise, Jim's handsome face was eight inches or so from her own.

"Merry Christmas," he said, his eyes twinkling with delight.

"Oh," Kate said, sitting up in her father's easy chair. She was surprised to see this man standing in her own living room. She thought it would have been so much better if her family had warned of a gentleman caller.

"Careful," Jim said, removing the glass from Kate's lap. After she'd fallen asleep, the drink had slipped from her hand and stained her robe with a wide, generous crimson discoloration.

"Sorry," Kate apologized, more out of habit than anything.

Jim sniffed the air around her. "You smell like you're about 80 proof right now," he joked.

Kate shrugged. "It's Christmas."

"So it is," he agreed. And with that, he whipped a gift from behind his back. "Here," he said cheerfully. "You left last night before I could give you this."

"Oh, wow..." She replied, genuinely surprised by the gift.

"It's okay if you didn't get me anything," Jim assured her. "We never really said we were getting gifts."

"Nonsense," Kate said emphatically, filling the air with wine-scented breath.

Jim drew back and covered his nose for a moment, as Kate stood and moved toward the stairs.

When she came back down, Jim had settled into the kitchen with Beth. The two were chatting casually, like long-time friends.

Oddly, it was at that moment that Kate remembered Beth's sweet and reassuring words from the night before. She smiled at her sister, then held out Jim's gift.

"Here you go," Kate said. After handing him his gift, Kate realized that she expected for him to take the gift and leave.

"Sit down, Kate," Beth directed.

Kate obliged, settling into the seat between Jim and her sister.

"I've been telling your sister about what happened last night. Tyke was way out of line. I really talked to him about his behavior."

Kate glanced at Jim's knuckles which looked scuffed, reddened and somewhat swollen. "Good," she told him.

Beth looked up from her phone and glanced back and forth from Jim to Kate, the two of whom seemed at a loss for words. Kate's hand was tracing the edge of a salt shaker, and Jim was thoughtfully squeezing his bottom lip between his thumb and forefinger. His eyes were on Kate, observing the young woman's every move.

For a moment, Beth considered leaving the kitchen. But instead she poked, "So are you two dating or what?"

Kate's neck snapped over to her sister, her eyes glaring. In years past, Kate hadn't minded Beth's tactless inquiries. *"Is that guy your boyfriend?" "What happened at the party?" "Who'd you make out with?"* Now however, it felt out of place, intrusive and harmful.

Kate heard Jim clear his throat as if preparing to answer.

"Well," he started, "I guess that depends on how this little lady feels," he finished, allowing his hand to rest lightly on Kate's knee.

"We don't have to answer her," Kate bravely corrected, straightening her posture as she did so.

"No, you really don't," Beth agreed. For all of the times she had probed and poked into Kate's affairs, she had actually never felt out of place or impertinent. She had simply taken advantage of her natural rights as an older sister. Or what had seemed like her rights at the time.

"Anyway, I'm going out myself,"Beth shared, almost defensively. She crossed her legs resolutely, feigning a false sense of confidence.

"Going out?" Kate repeated, genuinely surprised by her sister's admission.

"Yes," Beth replied, then finished, "Didn't I tell you? A while ago, I met someone."

"*You have?*" The three adults heard someone shout from the living room. "*Who?*" The disembodied voice belonged to their mother, Julia, a being who possessed supernatural hearing when it related to her daughter Beth, and her dating prospects.

"Yes, *Mom.*" Beth thought she would end the conversation there, but seeing the interest in Kate's face, Beth teased, "But it's not anyone you know."

Jim looked from Beth to Kate, and back again. Beth had a sweet face, pretty even, Jim thought. Not as pretty as Kate, but pleasant enough. Still, even as a newcomer, he could tell that Beth having a date must have been relatively uncommon.

"As a matter of fact, I think I'll start getting ready," Beth announced casually. Kate and Jim watched as Beth began to leave. Before exiting however, she touched Kate's shoulder and said, "Maybe you want to freshen up, too."

As if on cue, Kate's right cheek began to itch a bit. Fingering the edge of her face, Kate felt a scaly flakiness on her finger tips.

Her eyes closed as she realized the truth. She had never rinsed away the thick gray mud mask she had earlier applied.

Seeing her uneasiness, Jim smiled sweetly. "Don't worry. My mom wears them all the time."

Kate smiled.

"Speaking of which, my mom really liked you," Jim told her. "She thought you were sweet, the whole family did."

"Are they all really politically active like Tyke?" Kate asked.

Jim breathed deeply before answering, "Yeah, kind of. Not as aggressive as he is. But yeah, we're all pretty 'woke.' Speaking of which," Jim paused to slide Kate's present closer to her. "Here, open this."

Kate unwrapped the bright yellow paper and held up the contents. "Body wash," she said cheerfully. "Thank you."

"You just always smell so nice," Jim said. "So I thought you might like that sort of thing."

Kate smiled obligingly. "Well, I actually do have a gift for you, so give me a second."

Kate walked up the stairs carefully, thoughtfully. *Body wash*, she mused. For some reason her boyfriends always bought her body wash. It was as if they had all gotten some memo from the universe. *"Kate Hastings shall be gifted body wash. And wash for the body, shall Kate Hastings be gifted."*

Taking a moment to peek in the bathroom mirror, Kate saw the disaster she thought she would see; her skin looked as if she had become part lizard, gray and scaly. She stretched out her face to make the mask crack and splinter as much as possible before turning on the water. Then, instead of washing away the exhausted mask, Kate dried her hands and returned downstairs with the horrid looking mask in place.

Jim's eyes grew wide at Kate's appearance as she re-entered the kitchen. "It looks even worse now," he observed, partly amused, partly horrified.

Kate shrugged, "It's just a mask," she replied. "It won't last forever."

Jim shrugged in reply, and began to busily rip the paper from his gift. Seeing it, he felt initially disappointed, but tried to be cheerful. "Oh des box," he said, misreading the French label.

Kate smiled and shrugged. "Close enough."

"Okay, now close your eyes," Jim prompted. "I've got one more for you, but I didn't have time to wrap it."

Kate closed her eyes immediately, very pleased to be receiving two gifts. Feeling Jim place an object in her hands, Kate's eyes opened immediately. Jim's second gift was a book. Kate ran her hand over the smooth paper jacket, looking at the picture of the author on the back cover. The woman had a severe face, despite her attempt at a wide, toothy smile. Her hair was very straight and unfashionably long. She wore polyester pants that flared at the bottom. Her glasses seemed too large for her narrow face.

"Flip it over," Jim suggested, as if he suspected Kate needed instructions to do so.

Kate viewed the side of the book, then flipped it to its front to get the best look at the title. Upon reading it, her face fell into a sullen expression.

" 'Finding My Voice: The Beginner's Guide to Decision Making,'" she read.

Jim effused, "There's even a part about voting, and how you can decide *who to vote for.*" He smiled proudly, feeling as if he had gifted Kate not only a new book, but a new lease on life,--the quintessential guide to expanding her horizons. Jim reached out to touch Kate's small delicate chin, but feeling minorly repulsed by the tiny flakes of dried mud and dead skin cells that were dangling from Kate's skin, he opted to touch her shoulder instead.

His eyes were warm as he smiled gently. "You're welcome."

****

The make-up supplies in Beth's overnight bag were meager, much too meager she thought to help her achieve the major beauty overhaul she knew she would be attempting for this highly unexpected date. The man she planned to see that evening, Steve Taylor, was not exactly a hunk, but she personally found him very attractive. His deeply dimpled chin and grey-blue eyes made her feel faint whenever he was around. None of his students spoke of "Mr. Taylor" as a 'nice guy.' He was a fellow teacher with a reputation for yelling at his kids and referring to them as "boneheads." He seemed smart though, plus he was single. She and all of the other seventh grade teachers knew the state of his failing marriage from the many excitable phone calls he'd been constantly having with his then 'soon-to-be' ex-wife.

"They go at it *all* of the time," the art teacher had told her. "His class is right next to mine. It just goes on and on, every morning. I have to just close my door sometimes, just so I don't have to hear it. They're going through a divorce as we speak."

Beth had merely nodded, but said nothing. Secretly, she was desperately grateful to hear the news. She had been without a lover for so long, she thought someone would have to pry any eligible man out of her cold dead hands. Especially one with such a good-looking, intelligent face.

Their meeting had been so coincidental, completely unplanned. For reasons she did not agree with, her school district *mandated* her presence at the school even though the children were being taught virtually. Per the usual, the vast majority of teachers had vacated the building mere minutes after the end of the school day, but Beth had lingered behind. She spent some time sanitizing her room. She wasted more minutes staring idly out of the window. She sat in her chair and sent out mass emails to parents, reminding each of them to check their child's progress online. Then finally, she bundled up all of her belongings and headed for the elevator.

On a sudden whim, she had decided to grab a snack from the vending machine. Something salty, she thought as she pulled open the door to the teacher's lounge.
Upon entering the lounge, she recognized the figure sitting by the window immediately, despite the dimness of the lounge. Unmasked and resting comfortably in a cushioned seat sat Steve. His feet were boldly resting on the edge of the nearby windowsill, and his hands were casually folded and resting across his stomach. Hearing the door open, he swung his head around to see who was entering.

Seeing Beth's somewhat familiar, pretty face, he smiled and said quietly, "Look, it's starting to snow a little."

Beth dropped her belongings on one of the round tables and gasped quietly, more for effect than out of genuine amazement. If there was anything she was amazed by, it was that the man before her hadn't already been snatched up by one of the other single teachers in the building. Most of the teachers were married, but not *all*. She reached for her mask in the pocket of her cardigan. But seeing that Steve wasn't wearing protective gear, she decided to forgo hers as well.

Beth dropped coins into the snack machine, quietly, almost as if she was afraid she would ruin the special Christmas magic that was allowing her to spend these private moments with Steven. Alone. In the quiet, dimly lit room.

"Mind if I eat these here?" She asked quietly, holding up her back of plain chips.

"Nah, help yourself," Steve answered.

Beth opened her chips and nibbled them as delicately as she could. When Steve wasn't looking, she had quickly slid on a deep, purplish lipstick. She smoothed her hair quickly then resumed eating her chips.

"Been a long time since I just sat and watched the snow," Steve mused quietly, speaking more to himself than the woman near him.

Beth nodded in reply, even though Steve wasn't looking her direction.

Minutes ticked by in relative quiet. Beth's heart was pounding increasingly so. She felt she had been blessed by some wonderful Christmas angel with the chance to talk to a man she was so greatly interested in, but her brain was failing to think up even the slightest thing of interest to say.

"You're quiet," Steven observed, taking his feet down from the window.

Beth cleared her throat and finished chewing her chips, preparing to say something.

"That's alright by me," Steve informed her. "Gah, my ex-wife, I swear, all that woman ever did was talk. *Talk,"* he emphasized, "and *complain.*"

Beth chuckled. Realizing that he preferred her silence she quietly nibbled another chip instead of speaking.

"You teach ELA, right?" Steve probed.

Beth nodded in response, honored that he knew the slightest detail about her. She watched as Steve picked up a chair and placed it at her table before settling himself in the seat, barely nine inches from her own.

"I've got some of the kids you teach," he told her. "In my robotics club."

"Oh I forgot you were the sponsor," she said, speaking without meaning to do so.

Steve rolled his eyes, "Well, yeah. For the time being. I'm getting kind of sick of it. It's kind of weird now, with it being all virtual."

Without thinking Beth suddenly effused, "Oh no, you can't give it up. The kids love it. The robotics kids? That's all they ever talk about."

A slight smile began to shape Steve's lips, "Oh yeah?" he probed.

"Oh yeah," Beth continued, her passion for her students prompting her to advocate on their behalf. "And some of them,--how can I say it? They aren't necessarily the really *popular* kids," she explained. "Some of them get kind of picked on."

Beth was now looking directly into Steve's grey-blue eyes and speaking somewhat emphatically, though not rudely. She continued to effuse about her students and their eager involvement in the technology based club. But her nerve broke, as she gradually noticed how Steve's curious eyes were searching all over her body.

Beth blushed and finished quietly, "So, I've always just really admired you for doing that. For hosting the club and giving those kids, like, something kind of fun and cool to do. A cool club to belong to. It's..." Beth's voice trailed off as her nervousness increased. "It's beautiful," she finished, though she immediately regretted her choice of words.

Steve laughed loudly at her comment, filling the quiet room with the sound of his genuine mirth. As he laughed, he enjoyed the sensations that his own laughter caused to ripple throughout his body. Laughing had become a rare indulgence for him in recent months, during which time he and his wife had been finalizing their divorce. Beth's polite comment about his sponsorship of a kid's club seemed like an obvious overstatement to him. But as a man who was recently divorced and lonely, he felt uncontrollably ravenous for approval and admiration.

"Beautiful, huh?" he repeated, smiling again. Steve glanced over Beth's brown locks, allowing his eyes to trace around the smooth, full curve of her round cheek. He allowed his eyes to meet her own and saw that her stare was unwavering, intent, and deeply interested in him.

"Say, you know what? I'm probably gonna spend a good amount of time on my own over the holiday," Steve confided. "My kid's seventeen, and he's pretty hot to spend Christmas with his mom and her new boyfriend." Steve's voice grew tight as he shared the personal details, but he continued. "It might be kind of nice not to have to spend the whole holiday break by myself."

"Yeah, no, don't spend it alone," Beth added in, trying desperately not to seem too eager or hungry for love. Or *'thirsty"* as her students called it. Though as Steve's curious glance continued to swim and dance all over Beth, she felt tempted to wrap her arms around him and beg him to kiss her.

"Well that's what I'm saying," Steve asserted, his tone argumentative due to habit more than intention. "But I probably will, you know, spend it alone," he explained. "Unless I maybe find somebody I could hang out with."

At his words, Beth smiled and nodded. She reflected back to various magazine articles she had read over the years. What was it they had recommended to do when you wanted to lure a man? Blink playfully? Play with your hair? Her brain searched through ancient files in a desperate attempt to find the right move to make. It seemed to Beth that Steve was almost on the hook, if she could just load the right bait.

Then suddenly, Beth's subconscious mind urged her to gesture gently, alluringly. She rested her hand on

Steve's muscular knee and said quietly, "Christmas is all about finding friends to spend it with."

The move was sufficient enough to prompt Steve's next words, "Okay great. So maybe you can give me your number and maybe we can get together over the break."

"Okay, call this number," Beth said hurriedly, then excitedly rattled off her own phone number. When her phone rang, she instantly confirmed, "Okay, got it."

"Great," Steve said, then stood and told her, "I gotta get moving." He swung his chair around and swiftly pushed it beneath a neighboring table. "See ya," he called over his shoulder as he exited the room.

Beth had sat in the room feeling very lucky. No, *blessed*, she thought. It was just so wonderful to have finally spoken with him. To have finally started to get to know him. She clutched her phone hopefully in both of her hands, smiling softly as she did so. As she added Steve's info to her contacts, her fingers typed the details as if they had a mind of their own. Under the box labeled name, she watched her thumbs carefully type out, "Mr. Wonderful."

✱✱✱✱✱✱✱✱✱✱✱✱✱✱✱✱✱✱✱✱

It was either because Jim thought she was an idiot, or because she hadn't told him to take his book and stuff it. One of those reasons, she thought, was the reason she was low-key fuming at the moment.

Sure, it was sweet. On the surface. She realized she hadn't voted in what would mostly be the most important presidential race of her life. Plus, it was true, she probably had seemed like "a bland scoop of vanilla ice cream" at Jim's family's party. But did Tyke really have to humiliate her by saying it? She hadn't done anything *wrong*. She'd been polite. Nice. She had smiled and said sweet things about the children. She had made doubly sure not to offend anyone. Trish, Jim's mother had liked her. Why didn't Tyke? And now, what did Jim think of her?

Kate's eyes dropped down to peek at the book sitting beside her. The book stared back at her blankly, yet almost accusingly. *"Here I am,"* it seemed to say, *"Read me and get an opinion, already."*

Kate turned away from the book and reached to put on her boots. Jim had offered to take her out to an early dinner, and it seemed like a good idea. It was Christmas, but Beth was busily getting ready to go on her date. Her parents had snuck away into the bedroom and were happily sleeping off the rum they had enjoyed in the family eggnog.
As long as there was at least one place open, she was fine with just nibbling at a sandwich.

Kate's phone buzzed unexpectedly. She picked it up. To her surprise and minor disgust it was a message from Derek. The text included a picture of Derek and a group of his coworkers caught in a variety of playful and animated poses. The picture was labeled, "Merry Xmas."

Kate tossed her phone to the side without responding and slid on her other boot. When the phone buzzed again, she considered turning it off. Especially as she read the follow up text from Derek that read simply, "Miss your boobs."

6

ICE TO MEET YOU

Beth sped to her small house, and rushed into her bathroom. Her date with Steve began in just three short hours. She was panting as she searched through piles of make-up, years of accumulation. Her hands were shaking as she sorted glosses from eyeshadows from mascara. No date had seemed to her to be as important as this one, at least not for a very long time. There had been others, she recalled, as she used her hands to brush her loose strands of hair from her face. Dr. Tom Oliver, for instance, the balding academic who had made her feel stupid for having *only* earned her masters degree. And Jason Meranda, a smiling, beautiful man who had later revealed a much stronger desire for male company than for Beth's.

But this man, Steve, something about him screamed "The One," to Beth. Beth brushed her teeth fiercely, almost competitively. Perhaps it was because he had been married before. It proved to her that he was at least "the marrying type." Some men never get that far, never really intend on taking eternal vows. As

Beth wiped the corners of her mouth and stared deeply into her own eyes, she realized that this was her most dear dream. The home she owned, the car she drove, it was all secretly a part of the life she hoped to share with the man she loved. More importantly, with the man who loved *her*.

Time to stop daydreaming, she demanded of herself. As it were, she had barely been able to wrangle Steve into this date. During their chance meeting the teacher's lounge, Steve had said that he'd call her during the Christmas break. But quite frankly, he hadn't. On more than one occasion, Beth had considered calling him. But she knew better. In her experience, nothing made men run away faster than making them feel like you wanted them.

The night Kate had spent at her own apartment, Beth had milled around the house aimlessly. Her parents had been comfortably tucked into their living room watching an endless number of holiday films. Having found the person, her parents were "lucky in love." Beth dared to hope that her love "luck" was about to change.
As it were, she had made her own "luck," in securing her date with Steve. As she waited for Kate to return home, she imagined that her sister was wrapped in Jim's strong, passionate embrace. Beth could practically feel the kisses that she was certain Jim must have been covering Kate's entire body with. Kisses on her hands, her legs, her feet. Beth would have done anything to be locked in the same kind of heated, sexy embrace. It was that fantasy that spurred Beth to be daring in her own life. So, after pacing the floor of her childhood bedroom for several minutes, she decided to "accidentally," call Steve's number. She

thought it was possible that it would go to voicemail, in which case she figured she would leave a fun and lighthearted message, nothing that sounded too serious or demanding. She was formulating the magical message in her mind when Steve's voice interrupted her thoughts.

His tone had been polite, though not cheerful. Beth immediately regretted bothering him. What she didn't know, couldn't know, was that the divorced man had been drinking and was feeling somewhat somber, deeply lonely. He was more grateful to hear Beth's voice than what she knew.

Beth had apologized for calling, swearing that she had meant to send a text just to say "Merry Christmas," but that she accidentally called him instead.

Steve seemed unbothered by the details of her explanation. He slurred a bit that he would like to see her. He told her frankly that he was glad that she had called. "It's been really lonely over here," he admitted. "Christmas is hardly Christmas without a kid around."

Beth had listened to Steve's feelings and said polite, sweet things to comfort him. At a strategic pause, she inserted, "Oh I wish I was there to give you a hug."

Her suggestion stimulated the alcohol-dulled senses of the man on the other end. "Hey, weren't we supposed to get together?"

"Oh yeah," Beth said, feigning a sudden remembrance, "We were supposed to go out or something."

"Then let's do it," Steve told her. "Text me your address and I'll pick you up around seven...okay?"

To Beth, it had been more than okay. And when the car pulled up to her home, she was ready. Her makeup had created great holiday magic. She looked dark and sensuous, with dramatic, smokey eyeshadow and dark, faux eye-lashes, sprinkled with touches of glitter. Though it stung her eyes to do so, she had put on blue contacts to intensify the natural blueness of her eyes. Her lips were tinted a rich, luscious merlot. She was wearing the mask that her mother had made for her: a jet black spandex mask studded with glittering rhinestones. Her catsuit was form-fitting and daring. The body-shaper underneath was doing marvelous work along her waistline.

When she approached his car, Steve appreciated the deep 'V' of her neckline and the generous view it gave of her breasts. He smiled as Beth settled herself into his car. She thought she smelled the faint scent of beer as he complimented her.

"You look real nice, Betsy," Steve said, and then, barely looking at the road ahead of them, he pulled off into the street, a bit too far to the right, driving onto the edge of a neighbor's lawn before swerving out into the middle of the road.

Beth, feeling a sense of dread and nervousness, corrected him quietly, "It's Beth." She added quickly, "And wait please, I forgot something."

Obligingly, Steve put the car into park, allowing Beth to step out. The moment her feet hit the ground, her pulse pace slowed. Even though the night air was frigid, it felt good, even calming to her lungs. Taking a deep breath, she mustered all the courage that she had and walked to Steve's side of the car.

"Why don't I drive?" she cajoled, stroking Steve's arm soothingly. "You could sit in the passenger seat and just relax." She leaned near him; the smell of alcohol intensified.

Steve's slightly glazed eyes blinked slowly, taking in Beth's beauty. His mind was doing its best to consider her words. He was alert enough to know what she was implying, that he wasn't fit to drive. Wasn't capable.

Steve shook his head slowly, "I don't want you to worry. I can handle things," he said. "I'm a man, I've got things I can do. I can do things." He told her, his words and sentiments seemed logical to him. He didn't feel out of control, only relaxed. Less anxious.

Beth swallowed nervously, but smiled softly. "No, I know you're a man. You're a hell of a man," she agreed, trying desperately to reassure his ego. "And I really like you," she admitted. "I've been looking forward to this date so much. I really have." Her own admission caused her to choke up a bit, a reaction that surprised her. But it was a true thought, a genuine feeling. The candor of the sentiment wasn't lost on Steve, despite his slightly drunken state.

"I'm not drunk," he said.

"Okay," Beth agreed. "I'm not saying you're drunk, I just think I should drive."

"I'm not drunk, and you're very sweet Betsy. I love you," he told her. "You called me, and I was glad you called me. And I promise to take care of you." Steven reached out to touch Beth's hand. His hand was warm, his touch, surprisingly gentle. "I have all the things taken care of."

Beth took a moment to look at Steve. She had never noticed his Adam's apple before, but as his head lolled backwards toward his headrest, she noticed the Adam's apple, the thickness of his neck, and the small amount of chest hair that was playfully peeking out of his collar. His greyish eyes seemed to be pleading with her, announcing a need that was emerging from his soul. Feeling that he wouldn't mind her touching him, she reached out to stroke his forehead and allowed her fingers to trace through his dark hair. His temples were just barely kissed with strands of salt and pepper.

"God, you're beautiful," she whispered.

An approaching car slowly swerved around them. Though the driver of the car didn't honk, the hidden person drove closely enough to Steve's car that it was obvious the driver didn't appreciate Steve's awkward position in the road.

Beth leaned against the car and waved at the other car apologetically. Once the car had passed, Beth leaned back to Steve. She chewed her bottom lip nervously, but only for a moment. She swallowed tensely and informed her date, "I got all dressed up for you. 'Cause I wanted you to think I was pretty."

"I know," Steve agreed. "You look so nice. I think you look pretty."

"Right, but if you,--"

"I think you look pretty." Steve interrupted. "You look so nice. I think you're pretty."

Beth's eyes filled with tears, not from sadness, but a feeling of loss. She shook her head. "I really wanted to go with you tonight," then slowing the pace of her words, she added the ultimatum, "But if you don't let me drive, I don't think I can go with you."

"No," Steve said stubbornly. "No. You can't drive. I will drive. And I want to drive you."

Beth nodded. "Okay," she started, "Well I need you to be safe. But I can't go with you tonight. Okay? I can't go with you," she finished.

Steve nodded, as if he respected her decision. It was odd, to his thinking, that she would make such a big deal out of nothing. He was fine, and he knew it. Barely buzzed is how he would have described himself.

As Beth walked away, she took note of the make and model of his car. She tried to read his license plates through the clouds of tears in her eyes. The worst thing in the world was happening. Instead of being swept away for a night of romance and burgeoning passion, she was recording the license plate of a potential drunk driver and considering whether or not she should call the police. Her mouth twisted into a grimace and she realized the impact such a decision would have on their prospective relationship. He would never forgive her. Could you imagine, she thought, your date calling the cops on you? Then instead of finding new love, you get slapped with a DUI.

Beth turned slowly, deliberately and prepared to walk back into her house when she heard Steve honk the horn. She turned and saw Steve's keys dangling out of his driver side window on his forefinger. She paused for a moment, not wanting to misread the situation.

She watched as Steve stepped out of the car and walked over to Beth. "Okay," he said, "You win. You can be my chauffeur," he jibed. "I like you anyway. You're a good fish."

Beth laughed at his odd humor, unsure if it was his personality or the alcohol that was causing him to say odd things.

Walking slowly back to the car, Steve circled around to the driver's side door and opened it for her. "Ladies first," he reminded her.

Beth adjusted the seat and mirrors of the small sedan and waited for Steve to enter his car. As she waited, Beth enjoyed how the seats and interior of Steve's car smelled distinctly masculine. Clean, and warm but with the slight, exciting musk of Steve's cologne.

"Let's go!" Steve shouted cheerfully, feeling a sudden momentary burst of energy. Upon entering the car, he then fussed with the buckle of his seatbelt for a few moments longer than what should have been necessary. The task seemed to expend the last bits of

Steve's energy burst. Taking a deep, calming breath, he settled into the dark leather folds of the passenger seat and allowed the brave, pretty woman to his left to take control.

✳✳✳✳✳✳✳✳✳✳✳✳✳✳✳✳✳✳✳✳✳

"Come over this way!" Kate heard Jim shout. "You've got to get steady. Get steady on your feet!" Jim's laughter was breaking up his words. To both he and Kate's surprise, they had found an ice rink that was open to the public in the heart of downtown. Despite the limited number of fun things to do in the city, the rink was surprisingly unpopulated.

Kate was holding on to the edge of the rink and moving slowly and unsteadily. "Why don't they rent knee pads?" she hollered out. "I mean, not all of us are professional skaters."

Jim caught the general gist of her complaint, but had already glided many meters away from her on the ice. He hadn't ice skated for years, not since his hockey days. It was amazing to him how easily his body remembered how to give and sway, how to turn his feet, and how to brake. Kate on the other hand was not doing as well. He cut a few artful figure eights in the ice and then glided back over to Kate.

"Here, lean your weight on me," he insisted gently, taking hold of her elbow. Kate didn't yield control easily, however, as Jim tried to lead her. Her right, gloved hand was clenched tightly to the cold, *but secure,* railing.

"No honey," Jim cooed, soothingly, "You've got to let go. I promise, if you hold on to me, I won't let you fall."

Kate didn't speak or give a sign of agreement, but she did let loose of the railing. Jim wrapped his right arm around Kate's body and pressed her against himself tightly. As he led her around the rink, Kate felt lighter and looser. It was almost as if Jim was carrying her around the rink. As the minutes went by, she found herself feeling cheerier and more confident. It really was quite thrilling to be on the ice, even as the cold air and tiny bits of ice particles stung her face.

"I'm getting good at this!" She effused, though even she suspected that she was deluding herself.

Jim played along anyhow, glad to see that her mood was improving. "I was gonna say the same thing. You're practically ready to go pro."

Feeling encouraged by his words, Kate decided to be brave and branch out from her partner a bit. "Okay, just hold me by the hand," she suggested, and as she did so, she broke free from Jim's strong embrace.

"Careful," he warned quietly, not wanting to discourage his date's new found pluck.

"I got it, I got it," Kate insisted. "Let go!"

Though he thought it too soon, Jim relinquished his grip on Kate's hand as requested. He watched as she glided along slowly. She didn't seem to know how to speed up, nor slow down. She was working very hard to stay upright. Her arms were bent at the elbows and upright, as if she were surrendering to the police. She would awkwardly shift left or right without any natural grace or compensation. He shook his head disapprovingly, though he was greatly amused by her awkwardness. When they had spotted the rink, she had seemed so enthusiastic about skating. *That's so weird*, Jim thought, *because she's so bad at it*. Still, he was glad to be the man she was there with, glad to be good at something,--to have a skill he could teach her and perhaps impress her with.

As Jim watched his date, his thoughts distracted him from the reality that his awkward companion was slowly gaining speed. He wasn't far behind her though, which was a good thing.

"Jim..."Kate called, her voice rising at the end with a note of alarm. "Jim!"

Kate's call of alarm brought Jim out of his thoughts. It looked to him that Kate was speeding up, even without lunging or pushing forward. As the seconds went by, her motion was picking up velocity rapidly.

"Help!" Kate called out. Her forearms were still pointed upward as she slid toward the edge of the ice rink. The railing was actually less than two feet away, but Kate's inability to turn or control her body rendered the nearby railing useless.

Jim assessed Kate's situation and realized that the rink was slanted toward the ramp leading off of the ice. A skater with any amount of aptitude would have been able to grab the railing and carefully navigate the ramp. But Kate was inept on the ice, so unsteady. Jim clenched his teeth and sped past his date. He could hear Kate screaming as he whipped past her and swung himself into her path.

Landing into his hard body caused the air in Kate's lungs to escape with an "Oof." But as she quickly assessed her situation, she realized that she had been spared a very ugly fall down an uneven ramp that led to the cold, unforgiving concrete pavement.

Kate's eyes wandered upward from the pavement to Jim's shoulder to his reddened ear to the angles of his gorgeous face. Her heart was still pounding from her near fall, and she was still working to catch her breath. But she felt an additional exhilaration as well, an excitement stemming from having been saved by her handsome, athletic skating partner.

"I told you I wouldn't let you fall," Jim reminded her, his voice strangely raspy.
"Yeah, you did," Kate agreed, feeling somewhat enraptured. The closeness of his face to hers was exhilarating. His arms felt strong as they wrapped around her, holding her upright. Kate's hands clutched the fabric of Jim's coat as her eyes searched into his. The music of the skating rink had shifted from the cheerful tunes it had been playing earlier and had begun to play an ambient, peaceful instrumental version of O Come All Ye Faithful.

"Kate,..." Jim started, though he didn't know how he would finish. He only knew that he liked her an awful lot. Even more now that he realized that she was brave and adventurous enough to try new things. No one was perfect, he realized. But Kate was so much of what he wanted.

Feeling the sweet purity of the moment, Kate leaned her face forward and pressed her lips into Jim's. From the second that she kissed him, there seemed to be a light that shone between them. Some warmth, some peacefulness. A sweet togetherness that was defining and knitting them together. Kate's kiss lingered, but not lustfully so. She kissed Jim because he was nice, and because he liked her,--even when she was wearing an ugly face mask. She kissed him because he was the kind of guy who liked to watch Charlie Brown cartoons, and would rewind the movie for you if he accidentally skipped ahead. She kissed him because he had never gotten mad or testy, even as her sister Beth had scammed him out of a free Christmas tree. Jim was a nice guy, probably the nicest she had ever dated. *A gentleman.*

Pulling her face away, she opened her eyes and faced the man before her.
"I like you, Jim," she said simply, her voice warm and affectionate.
Jim smiled. "I like you too, Kate. I really do. You're pretty much,--" Jim stopped to gather his thoughts and swallow. He bravely decided to complete the thought, "You're pretty much the exact kind of girl I've always wanted to get to know. Pretty perfect. So,..." Jim's voice trailed off, but he then finished with, "I'm really honored that you would spend time with a regular guy like me."

Kate swallowed hard, utterly charmed by his words. Her eyes fluttered upwards as she considered his compliments. *Pretty perfect,* she replayed in her mind. Not once had any guy ever called her that. It had always been *"change this, or do that better."* Now, as she stood there in Jim's embrace, seeing tiny sparkles of ice float around the large, globe lights of the ice rink, Kate felt a thought break open in her heart,-- a thought as sweet and hopeful as the brand new, blushing light of dawn: Perhaps she had found someone who would like her, just as she was. Perhaps she had found a gentleman who wasn't shallow or weak. Or mean. A man who kept his word, stood up for what he believed in without crushing others. Perhaps she'd found...

"Hey," she started. "If I bought you something, *'just because.'* And it wasn't real expensive or anything, would you care? Would you want it or? Would you just, I dunno, leave it behind like it was nothing?"

Jim smiled, surprised by the oddness of the question. But seeing the seriousness in Kate's eyes, he answered earnestly, "I don't guess it would really matter what it was. If you bought it for me, that's what matters. At Christmas especially. That people love you and give you gifts from the heart, that's what matters to,--"

Jim tried to finish his thought, but he couldn't. The tender sweetness of his words had charmed Kate so much that her soft lips had pressed his own, now with more hunger, more certainty. Carefully, slowly, Kate's hands released their grip on Jim's sleeves. She stretched her arms out gingerly, and enrobed his body completely. Jim, thrilled by the feel of Kate's arms and warm body, kept his hands politely on Kate's waist, helping her to remain steady on the ice.

What a sweet and wonderful, girl, he thought. *What a wonderful girl.* As Kate pressed her face against Jim's chilled cheek, she enjoyed the slight grizzled feel of his 5'oclock shadow. She smiled, brightly and prettily as Jim stared into her soft blue eyes. The way she was looking at him made Jim feel as if he were slipping into a warm pool of light.

Kate stroked Jim's chin and nodded, giving herself approval to have a little faith, a little hope that the man in her arms was the one she needed in her life. And in that moment, she realized she felt better than she had in a very long time.

"Quite wonderful," she said aloud, her eyes closing peacefully. "Pretty perfect."

✱✱✱✱✱✱✱✱✱✱✱✱✱✱✱✱✱✱✱✱✱

"Well you're bad luck," insisted Steve. "You're jinxing this whole thing."

"No!" rebutted Beth, laughing at his insinuation. "How could it possibly be me that's bad luck. It's Christmas and the restaurants are closed. That's just how it is."

"That's *not* how it is," Steve slurred slightly.

"That is how it is." Beth returned.

"That's *not* how it is," Steve replied, "I've been living. I've been living in this town,-- this, my whole life," he told her, gesturing to the businesses of the darkened downtown area. "All my life these restaurants have been open, every Christmas. So now," he added, leaning his head closer to Beth, "Now if they are closed, it is definitely because of you."

Beth rolled her eyes, foregoing a reply. She smiled despite herself, sneaking peeks over at the man sitting in the passenger seat of his own car. His nose was somewhat pronounced, but only slightly hooked. *A*

Roman nose, she thought, imagining that perhaps he had been related to the emperors of ancient Rome. He had begun to chatter about something different, gesturing to various objects as they drove along. Each building they passed seemed to spark a new memory in him. This plus the Christmas spirits he had imbibed earlier were making him feel especially chatty and open.

"But that's when they had everything there, before Union Station closed down. 'Member that?" Steve probed. "They reopened, but it was closed down for a long time."

Beth nodded, pretending to be following the conversation.

"Then honestly, when it closed down, both me and my brother got kind of upset. 'Cause that was where we had had the best time with my mom."

Steve stopped speaking for a second and reached out to touch Beth's arm. "You didn't know my mom," he explained. "And she wasn't a good mom. 'Cause she couldn't be." Steve used the back of his finger to trace the softly curved outline of Beth's upper right arm. "She didn't know *how* to be," he continued. "She was just a girl. She got pregnant a couple of times. And that's just how it was." He took a moment to breathe before he looked out of the window and continued. "And my dad, well..." Steve swallowed. "He wasn't such a good dad. He spent most of his time in bowling alleys. Drinking beer and eating hot wings." Steve chuckled slightly, amused at his own words. "Me, I understood. I never really hated the guy. I just knew it was a messed up situation." Steve straightened himself, using chair controls to incline himself forward. "My brother hated him pretty much, but I never really hated him. I just felt it wasn't fair that he never told my mom that he was married while they were dating. But he was. He had,--" *burp* "he had a wife and three other kids."

Beth paused at a yellow stop light. She turned her face to Steve, searching his eyes out with her own.

"He was married?" She probed after a few moments. Steve had fallen silent. His eyes had closed and he was touching his stomach uneasily.

"Think I'm getting a little carsick," he said. A second later, he flung his door open and stepped out unto the sidewalk, rapidly emptying the contents of his stomach.

Beth peeked around via the car mirrors to see if they were impeding traffic. The light had turned green, but the one or two cars that drove near them seemed able to assess the situation sufficiently enough and simply swerved politely without so much as a blare of their horns.

Seeing that Steve was recovering, Beth stepped unsurely out of the car and made her was around to his side of the vehicle.

She was surprised to see tears in his eyes.

"I'm a mess, Beth," he told her, blinking slowly. "I was gonna take my kid out for a little time together. Like for a snowball fight. Or just whatever. But he didn't want to." Steve shook his head. "He was all hot to hang out with his mom and her new boyfriend. 'Cause the boyfriend's got money and he was promising Jake all kinds of stuff. Snowboarding, skiing. Crap like that." Steve pinched the corners of his eyes together, trying to collect himself. His lips trembled visibly. "*My* kid," he emphasized.

Instinctively, Beth placed her hand on his arm, massaging it gently. "He's just a kid," she comforted. "Probably just trying to have fun. Not even thinking about how you'd feel about it."

"Yeah I know," Steve agreed. "I don't think he was trying to hurt me. I just really didn't want to be alone this Christmas. And I didn't think *you* were gonna call. I had no idea," he confessed.

Beth watched Steve's Adam's apple move up and down as he swallowed and breathed deeply.

"So I had a few beers. Like a few too many. I was just gonna pass out. I haven't done that since my idiot years in college, Beth. *I swear.*"

Beth nodded. Something about the earnestness of his tone affected her deeply. Before her stood a beautiful man who had become, suddenly, horribly lonely. Though she knew others would have had many condemnations for his behavior, she felt too acquainted with loneliness and desperation to pass judgement. Beth smiled as she remembered Kate's sangria and the heavily laced eggnog she had been *over*-indulging in throughout the entire Christmas break. Though she was certain no one had noticed.

"It's just a hard time of year," she said, surprised by the tightness in her own throat. "It's better if you have a family of your own, a kid of your own,--stuff like that. At least, I think it is," she said, chuckling softly.

"You don't have any kids?" Steve inquired.

Beth shook her head. "Not yet. Trying to wait until, I dunno, everything's right."

Steve nodded. "You've just got to meet the right guy."

Beth nodded, uncertain about the meaning of his words. It was true, though, she agreed, regardless of Steve's foggy sentiment.

"Should I drive yet?" he asked her, "You wanna trade?"

"No, I'll drive," Beth assured him, walking back to the driver's seat.

Once tucked inside, Steve turned on the car radio. He enjoyed Christmas music greatly, though he had avoided listening to it until that moment.

He reclined his seat again and looked over to Beth's pretty profile. "We can go anywhere you want," he said.

Beth shrugged feeling somewhat dejected. His words, 'you just have to meet the right guy' was replaying in her mind, like a loop. Was he *not* the right guy? Was she wasting her time again?

"Hey," Steve said, his finger once again touching her arm. "I really am glad you called."

Beth focused on the traffic ahead of them and nodded.

"Hey something else," Steve started, "I've got a question for you."

Beth huffed, "What's that?"

"Are you the kind of person who only likes to go to like, *really nice* places? Or can you be comfortable in a place that's kind of more laid back. In maybe a not so great part of town?"

His words alarmed Beth slightly. The idea of going somewhere new intrigued her, but the thought of going to a "not so great" place unnerved her. "Someplace like where?"

"Okay," Steve sat up again, more alert and cogent having emptied the alcohol-based contents of his stomach. "Friend of mine has a place not too far from here. Sells really good bbq. Him and his family are selling plates for his cousin who got locked up." Steve paused for a moment, looking Beth directly in the face.

Beth paused, waiting to hear more. When Steve didn't continue, she probed, "Is that a big deal?"

"No. No, not to *me*," Steve said, smiling awkwardly, "I just didn't know if you had kind of,...I dunno know. Like, he's *my* friend and I like his whole family. But some people are kind of...judgy." Steve blinked and looked away. "I've known him since high school. A lot of his family is locked up. His dad. Older brother. A few cousins. But he's always been a real straight up and down guy."

Though driving, Beth took a few moments to cast a look in Steve's direction. "So, what you're asking me?"

Steve blinked his grey eyes at Beth, his dark lashes outlining their shape perfectly. "Nothing," said. "Just didn't know if you were kind of a, well, *snob.*"

"A *what*?" Beth laughed, feeling simultaneously shocked, offended and amused. "Me? A *snob*?"

"I mean 'cause look how you're dressed," Steve protested. "You're wearing like a fancy dress."

"Black velour catsuit. With matching blazer," Beth corrected.

"And I'm just wearing jeans. And a sweater." Steve paused as he watched Beth turn into a parking lot. She reasoned it would be best to stop driving for a moment until she knew where exactly they were going.

"I'm not trying to offend you," Steve demurred, his voice and tone softened.

"No, I'm sure you're not trying to offend me," Beth agreed. "Just probably still drunk."

Following Beth's accusation, an uncomfortable silence quickly settled them. Beth braced herself for Steve's retort, certain that he would return her insult.

Instead, he replied calmly. "Promise I'm not still really drunk. And I swear I wasn't trying to offend you. I just noticed how nice you look. You always look pretty, and neat and well put-together."

The compliment charmed Beth immediately. She hadn't expected one, especially at that moment. She blushed, though she didn't want to let on how affected she was by his words.

She cleared her throat. "Well, two things. I'm not a snob, and I'm not 'the pretty one.' Not really, "she informed him. "My sister Kate is gorgeous. She's blonde. Really thin. Nice knockers," she said, laughing at her own words. "She's sort of always been the pretty one between the two of us." Subconsciously, Beth began to peek at herself in the rearview mirror.

Boldly, Steve reached over to touch Beth's chin. His hands were slightly cool compared to the warmth of her face. She recoiled from surprise only slightly, but then allowed his cool fingertips to gently cup her chin.

"I've always sort of liked brunettes," Steve confessed. His eyes trailed over her dark hair, admiring the gentle swirl and twist of her soft waves. His admiration of her beauty increased as he took note of the blueness of her eyes and the exotic contrast they made with her mink-colored locks.

His voice was breathy but earnest, "No, *you're* the pretty one."

Beth swallowed audibly. In her mind there had been moments, mere moments when she had dreamed, *fantasized* that someone would see her and say those words. That she was the pretty one. But it had never happened. She loved her little sister, truly wanted the best for her. But Beth wanted one, just *one* man to look at her with favor and preference. A man who wanted her above all other women. At that moment, she swore that if Steve would look at her that way...

"Do you think I'm beautiful?" She inquired boldly.

Steve laughed. The sound was unapologetically loud and sharp. It resounded inside the tiny compartment.

"Yeah," he admitted. "Really good-looking face. And a nice figure too. 'Cause I've always kind of liked girls with, uh, *'a little junk in the trunk*,'" he said, referring to Beth's ample backside. Despite the chilled weather, she had dared to bare a generous amount of cleavage. Though now with Steve's eyes observing and appreciating the feather soft curves of her breasts, Beth felt somewhat naked and vulnerable.

"Hey," Steve said, "What about me? Am I beautiful?"

Beth tinkled in laughter, surprised by his question. She nodded. "Very."

Steve nodded in response. He drew in a deep, audible breath, then blew it out slowly toward the front window which was beginning to steam up. His eyes turned back to Beth who was biting her lip expectantly. He knew that she wanted him to kiss her. But he didn't feel prepared to do so, yet. He really did like her. She seemed smart. And nice,--just the kind of person he'd want to become involved with one day. But he wasn't sure if he was completely ready to date.

His marriage was over. He had accepted that. Regardless, he knew he was still 'getting himself together,' and Beth just didn't seem like the kind of woman he'd want to mess around on.

Steve smiled at her gently, reassuringly, seeing the hunger in her eyes. Though he wasn't sure how far he felt prepared, he knew for certain that he was very glad to have met her, pleased to be in her company. He reached up gently pushed her hair behind her ear.

"Let's go get some bbq."

7

HOT, FRESH GINGERHEAD

It hadn't been said, exactly, *not yet*. However, both Jim and Kate could feel it. This was the beginning of something special. The beginning of *them*. Kate snuggled herself against Jim, holding on to his arm as they rode along in his pickup. Truthfully, the position of her body felt somewhat awkward with the seatbelt straining against her waist and neck. Jim seemed a little uncomfortable too. He was driving with one hand, but was obviously accustomed to driving with two. Regardless, the two seemed happier awkwardly snuggled in Jim's front seat than if they had allowed even so much as eight inches to separate them.

"You hungry?" Jim asked quietly, suddenly feeling instinctively provisional for the woman lovingly wrapped around his arm.

Kate smiled and nodded. "Just a bit noshy, though." She traced the outline of Jim's cheekbone with her finger. Jim turned his head suddenly and playfully caught Kate's fingertip between his lips.

Kate squealed with delight and surprise. She withdrew her hand back to herself and kissed his cheek. Smiling, she settled back into position, wrapped adoringly around Jim's arm.

"Are *you* hungry?" Kate cooed.

Jim sighed deeply. Then, though he was not often the kind of man to openly share his feelings, he confided. "No not really. I don't really want anything else in the world right now." Though they were driving on a highway that was surprisingly busy, he chanced a glance at Kate and continued. "To be honest, Kate. I've been looking for a girl like you my whole life. Someone sweet. Beautiful. Classy." He paused. "I just think of you as the kind of girl that probably every guy wants to marry."

Kate smiled and pressed her face against his shoulder. She kissed Jim's shoulder and whispered. "Thank you."

Jim had pulled up the sleeves of his hoodie, revealing his hairy, muscular forearms. Kate's touches were light and sweet as they dotted and brushed his skin. Her touch was playful, yet enticing.

Then feeling her stomach escalate quickly from noshy to actively hungry, she decided that she definitely wanted a bite to eat. Forgetting momentarily how uncomfortable her last visit had been, Kate chirped. "Hey, how about we stop in at Max's? She's actually usually open on Christmas. I know she will be this year, because the economy has been kind of rough."

Jim continued to drive, his eyes never wavering from the road.

A minute of silence passed between the two.

Suspecting that perhaps her question hadn't registered, Kate repeated her suggestion, now in question form. "What do you think about going to Max's? Wanna see if she's open?"

Jim's face flattened to a non-emotional stare. He licked his bottom lip. He swallowed.

"Babe?" Kate probed, then feeling a bit silly for having used such a loving epithet, started again. "Jim?"

In a quick moment, Jim crossed two lanes to make it to an exit ramp they were rapidly approaching. Kate's body tightened instinctively. She gripped the door handle of the truck and held her breath.

As Jim reached the top of the exit ramp, he made an urgent, though less manic left turn. A moment later he pulled safely and calmly over to a gas station, well populated with masked persons flowing in and out.

"Here you go," Jim offered politely. "This is a good place. They've got hot dogs, pizza, donuts. Anything you want, really." Then looking Kate over, he smiled and added, "Salads and water, too."

Kate nodded.

The two wrapped their faces in masks, the gesture taking only a few seconds with the two having become so practiced at the act.

Upon entering the brightly lit gas station, the attendant took a moment to holler out a greeting to Jim while in the middle of completing a complicated transaction.

"I sort of come here a lot," Jim confessed, laughing at the truth.

Kate nodded.

"Salads are over there," Jim said hurriedly, pointing in the direction of a cooler. "I gotta use the restroom. B-R-B." He kissed Kate on her cheek and darted away.

Kate milled around the gas station, arms folded tensely. The place actually had a surprising array of foods to eat. She found the salads, and the donuts. Though she forced herself to forgo the latter.

Seeing that there were a couple of two-person tables available for sitting, she grabbed a fresh paper towel, wet it with hand sanitizer and wiped their table and chairs.

Jim appeared after a few moments. "Pssst!"

Kate responded to the sound and glanced up to see Jim smiling and waving her over. Kate stepped over slowly, "Yes?"

"D'you see the salads? They've got everything, don't they?"

Kate nodded. She swallowed and prepared to ask Jim a question that she did not feel prepared to hear the answer to.

"Step over," a grimacing cashier commanded.

Tenderly, Jim clasped Kate's elbow and ushered her toward the counter. Jim paid for the bundle of snacks in his hand, which included a tasty looking chef salad he had thoughtfully picked up for Kate.

Having completed their transaction, the two sat at the seats Kate had cleaned.

"My mother really liked you," Jim started. "I'd been meaning to tell you that. My dad, too. But really, he likes your whole family."

Kate nodded and gave a tiny smile, "I like your parents, too. Your mom Trish was really nice." Kate looked away, but remembering the old man and woman she'd seen at his parents home, she inquired. "And the elderly couple that was there, were they your grandparents?"

"Yes!" Jim exulted. "Yes, that was them in the flesh. We hardly ever get them to leave their house anymore, so it was kind of a big deal that they were there." Jim paused to rip the corner edge of a plastic wrapper off with his teeth. Spitting the paper bits out unceremoniously, he quickly added, "I should have introduced you. Did you get a chance to speak to them?"

Kate shook her head in reply. "No, no. I didn't bother them. Your grandmother was fixing your grandfather's blanket. So, I don't know. I didn't want to disturb them."

Jim's voice was soft as he assured, "They wouldn't have minded. My grandmother is as sweet as pie. Granddad is too,--*these days*. He was a bit of a drill sergeant when we were younger. But since his health has been declining, he's been pretty mild. Stays pretty quiet."

"I see," Kate said, nervously fingering and tapping the edge of her salad.

Jim joked, "You gonna eat that, or just thump it?"

For the first time in several minutes, Kate looked straight ahead and actually looked Jim in the eyes. His face looked pleasant, earnest and unassuming. His eyes were smiling at her in obvious adoration.

Kate acquiesced. "Yeah, let's eat." She ripped open the plastic packaging and began mindlessly poking her salad with a fork.

Carefully, Jim stretched out his fingers and pressed them to the back of Kate's hand, urging her to pause. "Let's say grace. *Together.*"

****

Sitting in the parking lot of a used car dealership, Beth lifted a forkful of the best potato salad she had ever tasted in her life.

"Good, isn't it?" Steve asked her, amusedly. "I know. His whole family can cook like that."

"I can't even imagine," Beth returned. "I'd be big as a house." She looked around herself, observing the people near her. Many were young, early twenties, she figured. They were beautiful young people. The girls had unbelievable curves, with such tiny waists. The young men seemed exuberant, quite loud, but largely harmless. Most of them were flirting or standing in groups with friends. About a third of them were without a mask, but Beth tried not to judge. She was tired of wearing her own mask, but still insisted on standing at least six feet away from anyone she didn't know.

Except Steve.

He was eagerly forking the food and shoveling it into his mouth. He had a ravenous appetite she noted. With his cheeks puffed out like a squirrel's stuffed nut pouches, he looked up at Beth and winked.

Seeing the ridiculous amount of food he had placed in his mouth, Beth joked facetiously, "I'll give you a thousand bucks if you can name all fifty states in the next ten seconds."

Steve began to laugh heartily which caused potato salad to slip from his mouth. He covered his face with his hands and turned away in order to recover. Wiping his face with a napkin, he laughingly accused, "That wasn't cool."

Laughing, Beth admitted, "You're right. I'm sorry."

"Nah, it's okay," Steve told her. "Actually feels really good to laugh." He paused to look at his pretty dinner companion. "You're smart, too, aren't you, Beth? And you've got a fun sense of humor."

Beth blushed freely. She couldn't remember any other date who'd been so polite and complimentary. Well, a few, she recalled, but all those dates with their compliments had sounded syrupy. Campy. The kind of compliments a seducer would lay on thick when they have an end goal in mind. She wasn't proud of the mistakes she had made in the past. But she was glad they were in the past. Here with Steve, she felt she was in the company of a gentleman. Sure, he had shown up drunk and had all but accused her of being a racist, but other than that, he was a pretty nice guy.

"Y'all want some more? We 'bout to close up and my grandmother is giving the rest of the food away."

The couple turned to see a young woman speaking to them. Her face was a deep, fudge brown and her skin looked smoother than moonlight. Beth thought she looked underdressed, wearing only a hoodie and a scarf.

"No, we're good," Steve answered for them. "But tell Ms. Patterson that everything was wonderful. I hope Tyrell gets out soon."

The young woman nodded and reached for their plates. "I can throw that away for you," she offered.

"Thanks Sweetheart," Beth said, though before she extended her plate to the generous young woman, Beth used her thumb to scrape off the last of the sweet and savory potato salad, wondering if she'd ever have a chance to taste it again.

Steve took a final swig of the beer he had ordered. Swallowing a mighty mouthful of the beverage, he burst out, "Alright, let's go!"

Beth nodded. "So I'm still the designated driver?"

"Yep," Steve agreed, softly chuckling aloud. "I don't get the chance to get chauffeured around too often. I'm taking advantage of it. Besides," he cajoled, "It's Christmas. So you can't judge."

To Beth's surprise, Steve suddenly took her by the hand and began waltzing around the parking lot.

Beth blushed in embarrassment. Though few people bothered to look in their direction, she felt that they were making a spectacle of themselves.

"Steve, people are looking," Beth whinged.

Steve shrugged, "So? Let 'em look. Doesn't matter." Then taking a peek around, he realized that they were perhaps more visible than what was necessary. "Here, come with me," he directed. He began walking toward the side of the building.

Beth stepped carefully along the broken concrete and bits of frozen ice covered grass, allowing Steve to lead her to the darkened side of the dealership.

"Here, is this better?" He asked quietly, his arms being to drape around Beth's waist.

"Well yeah, 'cause no one can see us now," Beth giggled.

Steve shook his head. "Don't live your life looking for someone else's approval, Beth-y," Steve instructed, spontaneously adding the new nickname to his sentiment. "Just be you."

Beth nodded, enjoying the feel of Steve swaying her gently. She looked up to find Steve staring at her. His gaze intensified as she stared up at him.

His voice was quiet as he confessed, "I'm not a perfect person, Beth. I've got some stuff to figure out. But..." His voice trailed. "But," he continued. "I know when I've found a good thing." He lifted Beth's hand over her head and twirled her in a circle like a ballerina. Beth laughed, trying to turn gracefully.

Steve, delighted by the look of sheer happiness on Beth's face continued to spin her slowly. The spins pushed them toward unsalted pavement.

"You're a pretty good dancer," Steve lied.

Beth, feeling alighted by his flattery and the sweetness of the moment, waved her hand elegantly and prettily, She then tried to do a small pirouette. Unfortunately, her high-heeled foot had found a small patch of black ice. Without the grace and balance to catch herself, she slipped very quickly and heard a crunching sound as she hit the ground.

Beth yelped in pain.

Steve yelped in panic.

They both seemed to know that this was *'not good.'*
****

Kate munched her salad thoughtfully, listening to Jim chatter about the various things on his mind. He had become quite the chatterbug, attempting to amuse her with stories of his days as a hockey player. His antics in youth choir. Memories of his family and grandparents. Kate tried to take it all in. But she couldn't shake the persistent needling suspicion in her mind.

As the minutes ticked by, Kate felt a familiar sense of disappointment overcome her again. The feeling only intensified as Jim talked nonstop. She could tell that he was attempting to fill the space between them with words, never leaving a gap or space where she could ask her own question or pose a doubt. Her eyes and throat began to feel tight, and she knew she would cry soon. The difference, she felt, was that this time,--this very first time, she didn't *want* to cry. She didn't want to fall apart. She just wanted the truth.

"So what happened with Max?" Kate cut in, her voice sounding sharper and louder than she had intended. She made no apologies for her tone, however. She only waited for Jim's reply.

Jim seemed to visibly melt in the seat before her. He took a moment to finger the small nut caught between his teeth, searching for the right words to say. How much was too little, how much was too much? He wasn't the kind of guy to sleep around, didn't find himself in awkward situations like this very often. And he liked Kate, really liked her. He thought it would be best to lie.

That evening with Max hadn't meant very much to him. He felt that it had meant even less to Max, who had left that same night and never returned any of his texts. He had stopped into Max's cafe to get another bowl of soup and coffee. He did think Max was pretty, appreciated her sense of political awareness and call to action. The two had chatted and agreed to go for a walk after the cafe closed. Before the walk had ever occurred, Max had saddled him in his car, undressing and kissing him urgently. He had never had a woman be so forward. Never been kissed with such a ravenous appetite. It had crossed his mind to push her away. But in truth, he'd greatly enjoyed the feeling of being desired. Max had been a thunderstorm, a rock star, a redheaded fury that claimed him passionately. But the fury and passion had only lasted one night. And afterward, he felt discarded. Unwanted. Rejected.

Now looking into Kate's eyes, it seemed impossible to relay these feelings. Jim shrugged, "Just, I dunno. Some things happened, I guess."

Kate nodded, feeling a hot anger rise in her chest. " *'Some things happened,'* " she repeated back. "Meaning you had sex with her."

Jim swallowed hard. Instinctively, he began to defend himself. "Well she was coming onto me pretty hard," he insisted. "I mean, even in the cafe that one time, didn't it seem like she was flirting with me pretty hard?"

"Yeah, I saw her flirting," Kate admitted. "But I didn't know you'd slept with her. That I didn't know." Kate gathered her coat quickly. It whipped like lightning as she pushed her arms through her sleeves. "*That*, I didn't know."

"Kate, please don't let this ruin everything. I mean the way the whole thing happened,--"

I'm not letting anything ruin anything, Kate thought. She took out her cell phone and prepared to call Beth for a ride home.

"Kate, I'm sorry," Jim gushed. "I would have told you. But then again, when? I mean it's only been tonight that we've sort of decided...I mean, didn't we decide tonight to be official?" Jim felt ridiculous asking the question, especially with the look of hurt and fury on Kate's face.

"Please Kate, just say something," he pleaded.

"Shut up," she replied, looking through the series of missed calls and messages on her phone. "And take me to the hospital. My sister's been in an accident."

The ride to the hospital was somber and tense. Once at the hospital, Kate jumped out of Jim's vehicle, and attempted to enter the emergency room.

"My name is Kate Hastings. I'm here to visit my sister."

Kate's urgency was met with flat indifference as nurses and security began to point at various signs and prattle off the emergency Covid-19 protocol. Kate closed her eyes in resignation as she was subjected to a flurry of temperature and symptom screenings.

"Fill this form out, too. And who are you here to see, sir?" a nurse asked Jim.
In her urgency to get into the building, Kate had failed to look behind her. She didn't expect to see *him* still standing there.

"I just wanted to make sure this lady got in alright," Jim said, gesturing to Kate.

The nurse's tone was sharp and unyielding. "Okay, well you cain't block the doorway, sir."

"Yeah," Kate chimed in, "You can't block the doorway. So, you may as well go home."

Jim nodded and stepped away, disappearing into the flurry of lights and ambulances.

"She was admitted about 10 minutes ago." The nurse informed Kate. "Does she have a visitor with her?"

"I don't think so," Kate offered.

"Okay, well if she does, they'll send you back out. Please perform hand hygiene upon entry and exit of the patient's room. Room 5."

Kate adjusted her mask and moved quickly as the door buzzed to allow her entry. She braced herself for what she might see. There was no way to know how much damage the accident had done to her sister. She was moving quickly and missed her sister's room.

"Kate!"

Kate stopped and backtracked quickly to an open door. There her sister lay, smiling. Besides the smeared mascara around her eyes, looked quite whole and in a particularly good mood. She wouldn't have looked injured at all, except for leg which was elevated and wrapped in bundles of ice packs.

Kate breathed a sigh of relief, though her nerves were still a bit on edge. "Okay," she exhaled. "So I can see you're pretty much in one piece."

"Yes I am," Beth agreed. "But look, they've got a one visitor only policy. And I knew you were coming, so try to hide a little if the nurses come."

"Why?" Kate asked, "Who else is coming."

As if on cue, Steve slid back into Beth's hospital room. He had been hiding in the bathroom just down the hall, evading the attention of the overly busy nurses. In a hushed voice, he informed Beth, "I think I gave that mean one *the slip.*"

Beth covered her mouth with her hands as she laughed at Steve's antics, forgetting that her face was already covered by a mask.

Seeing a new person in the room, Steve asked, "Hi. Who's this?"

"This," Beth informed him, "is my baby sister Kate."

Steve took the blonde woman in, expecting to be bowled over by her beauty. By the way that Beth had described her, he anticipated a mix of Marilyn Monroe and Helen of Troy. Feeling a bit underwhelmed by the woman, he decided that she must be prettier without her mask.

"We got here in an ambulance," Beth shared, offering the tidbit as a way to stimulate conversation. "That was my first time in an ambulance."

"Yeah, they wouldn't let me ride with her because we aren't married or 'cohabitating'," Steve shared. "Stiff protocols."

"What kind of accident did you have?" Kate asked, ignoring the man beside her and focusing on her sister.

"A dancing accident," confessed Steve, which sent Beth into a fit of silent giggles. Steve laughed as well, his usual loud sounding guffaw, which he suddenly felt afraid would alert the nurses to his presence.

"A dancing accident," repeated Kate, interrupting the delighted giggles of Beth and Steve. "And you needed to take an ambulance." Kate turned her eyes to the man in the room. "Why didn't *you* drive her?" she interrogated.

"Oh. Well..." Steve's face sobered a bit as he prepared to share candid information regarding his indulgences in alcohol that evening.

"Well, we'd both been drinking," Beth lied. "So, we just thought it was best to call an ambulance."

"Oh, so you were drunk." Kate's accusation was a missile directed solely at Steve.

"Not very," Steve generalized. "I mean, a bit, I guess."

"We were on a *date*, Kate," Beth defended. "People drink on dates."

"Right, so who was driving?" Kate asked. Then turning her attention back to Steve, she grilled him with, "So you took my sister dancing, got so drunk that you couldn't even drive her to the hospital, and why? What were you trying to do? Date rape her?"

"Kate!" Beth called out. "Are you crazy? We were on a *date*. We just, I guess we just got carried away."

"No," Steve confessed. "It really was me. Beth wasn't drunk. I was drunk. I showed up drunk." Steve cast a mild smile in Beth's direction. "But your sister took great care of me tonight." Steve's face seemed to lose a bit of color as he confessed. "I do feel bad about it, though, Beth."

"You should feel bad," Kate agreed.

"Oh my Lord," Beth interrupted. "Kate,--"

"No, she's right. Plus," Steve said, grabbing his coat. "I better get out of here. I don't want that nurse to come back and chew me out again for not washing my hands appropriately."

Beth smiled at Steve before throwing darts of rage at Kate.

"I'll call you tomorrow," Steve comforted. "Got a buddy of mine coming to pick me up. See you later, Alligator." Steve shot double finger guns at Beth just for extra cheesiness, making Beth chuckle, yet again. He turned to go, leaving Beth to watch him disappear down the hall.

Kate rolled her eyes and sat in the seat beside her sister's bed, ignoring the look of pure disdain Beth was giving her.

To both of their surprises, Steve suddenly re-entered the room. "To hell with the rules!" he announced. He quickly removed his own mask, then pulled down Beth's mask as well, revealing her lips which were still stained a pretty purplish color. Steve leaned in quickly, then paused to search out Beth's face. Seeing no objections, he pressed his lips to hers and enjoyed the soft warmness of her mouth. Her lips were trembling the slightest bit, both from surprise and excitement. She was thrilled to be kissed by him, even while reclining in a hospital bed. His lips were soft and cushy. They covered her mouth completely.

Steve stood erectly and returned his mask to his face. "Okay, really leaving now. Bye ladies."

Beth waved goodbye, feeling young and giddy as Steve left her bedside. Kate, on the other hand, looked uncomfortable and dejected. Her eyes lifted suddenly.

"Guess you guys hit it off, huh?"

Beth nodded, but seeing the tears forming in her sister's eyes, she felt prompted to ask, "How did it go with Jim?"

Kate didn't answer. Instead, she reached for the remote control and started flicking through the boring options available via the hospital's cable service. The sisters watched a hopeful update regarding the increasing availability of Covid-19 vaccines, before settling on an old episode of Scrubs.

"Ha. I wish hospitals were that cool." Beth said. In the moments that passed, the girls laughed together and ultimately relaxed. But during a commercial break, Beth touched the remote, rendering the television silent.

"Talk," she ordered.

Kate shrugged and allowed the tears that she had held back earlier to flow freely.

"Jim slept with Max."

Beth's eyes widened in surprise, but she remained silent.

Kate continued, "I thought he was the one. Thought he would be different." She wiped her face with the back of her hand. "But! It turns out that just a couple days after meeting me, he decided it would be a good idea to bang Max's brains out."

At this point, Kate's cries were becoming intense. She laid her head down on her sister's hospital bed. Beth stroked Kate's hair and unmuted the television,-- both as a distraction and to mask the sounds of her sister's grief, which Beth felt was no one else's business. The girls watched tv and held hands until their father came to take both of his beloved daughters home.

8

YOUR CHANCES ARE JIM TO NONE

The next day found Kate feeling stronger and more balanced than the previous night at the hospital. Though things hadn't worked out with Jim, Kate felt oddly confident and focused.

The family had pulled out an old wheelchair from their garage, and plopped Beth into it. The pain of the torn knee ligament as well as the sprain in her ankle was immobilizing. Regardless, Beth strained to roll and navigate the house independently, even daring to put a small amount of weight on her ankle.

When her sister Kate caught her in the act, Kate felt a novel sense of unapologetic forcefulness overtake her. "Sit. *Down*," she commanded, her fists resting on her hips.

"I'm fine," Beth argued. "I just have to,--"

"You just have to sit there. And rest. And let me or mom know if you need something." Kate informed her. "That's what *you* have to do."

Beth stared at her sister with open rebellion on her face. "You're not the boss of me," Beth mumbled.

"Oh yeah I am," Kate countered. "Especially since you've decided to date drunk guys who can't even manage to take you to the hospital."

"No," Beth demurred, "You don't even know him. It was Christmas. His kid left him. He got divorced recently. It's just been a really rough time for him," Beth sympathized, flicking through her phone messages to see if Steve had sent her another message. He had been texting her all morning, sending pics of his house, random objects he'd found at the grocery store, and quite a few pictures of his dog, *Crunchy*. Beth had never felt so immediately "involved" with someone.

"Yeah, I'm sure he's a real winner," Kate quipped. Seeing an Amazon truck outside, she stepped away to answer the knock on the door and retrieve the package,--something she imagined was a late Christmas present.

Instead, it was Jim holding the family's package. Kate watched the delivery truck drive away.

"Give me that. What do you want?" She demanded.

Jim paused before answering. "To say I'm sorry." After a moment, he gestured toward his pickup. "Also, you left your scarf, your iPod and some other stuff in my truck."

Kate stepped past Jim and marched to his truck. To her frustration, the door was locked.

Jim approached from behind carefully, closely. The closeness of him was disturbing to her. He was wearing the cologne she had bought him for Christmas. He smelled of cedar, pine and warm spices. His steamy breath brushed her neck.

"Hurry up," she barked.

When the door opened, Kate tossed Jim's property around rudely, while attempting to find her own belongings.

"Can we at least talk about it? Like adults?" Jim probed.

Snatching her scarf from his front seat, Kate snarled, "No, we cannot. There is nothing to talk about. You're just a total disappointment as a human being," she told him.

Jim swallowed and rolled his eyes, "Seems a bit harsh."

"I don't care," Kate countered. "I'm so sick of men and the way you guys behave," Kate threw her full weight into the truck door to shut it. "You can't just treat people like they don't matter!"

"I agree," Jim agreed. "Which is exactly how Max treated me, just so you know."

"Oh, cry me a river," Kate snorted. "That's what you get for sleeping with somebody you knew for like, ten seconds."

Jim's face grew angry at the accusation. "I didn't say I was proud of it."

"And what exactly was so great about her anyway?" Kate demanded. "Are you just really into redheads? You see a pretty girl and your pants just automatically hit the floor? Men are such sluts."

Jim's eyes narrowed. Kate was throwing haymakers, daring him to toss out a few of his own. "No, I don't just sleep with anybody, red-headed or not," he corrected. "But I liked Max because she seemed energetic and interesting. She *reads*, for crying out loud. And she's got *actual opinions* about things,-- things that matter," he continued. "And I guess I did like that about her. She didn't seem afraid to speak her mind or stand up for what she believes in. That sort of thing."

Kate's eyebrow raised in objection to Jim's implication. "You think I'm afraid to speak my mind?" she asked.

"You seem like it," Jim goaded, aware that he had hit a nerve.

Kate tossed her scarf around her neck as if it were a cape. She placed her hands on her hips and leaned in closely to Jim's face.

"You know what, I *am* afraid to speak my mind," she confessed. "Because people like you, and Max, you guys make *everyone else* feel like what we think or say is so wrong. If we don't say the *exact* right thing, at the *exact* right time, to the *exactly* right people we get shot down or slapped with some kind of label."

Jim's eyebrows furrowed as he listened to Kate, trying to discern her meaning.

Kate continued, "I mean sure, I get it. Max is all political. She went to some marches and she's got the matching t-shirt. But that doesn't mean she cares more about people than I do. I care about people," Kate insisted, pointing toward her own heart. "I care about people."

Jim nodded. "I'm sure you do."

"No I *mean* it," Kate stressed. "But when I say I care about people, I mean I care about *all* people. Black lives, white lives, blue lives, cat lives. *Everybody matters.* And sure, yeah, I get it." Kate said, nodding emphatically. "When people are being hurt, we *all* have to stand up. I wanna do that, too. I wanna be a part of the solution, even though I have absolutely no idea how to do that," Kate informed him. Her lips were trembling as she dared to voice things she had never said before.

Jim folded his arms, deciding to listen instead of respond. Kate didn't seem very practiced in expressing herself, so he thought he would let her emote without interrupting. "Go on," he prompted.

"Okay, I will." Kate agreed. "I mean, for crying out loud, I used to date a Black guy. *Derek.*" Kate rolled her eyes and continued. "And even he used to tell me that sometimes the cops do bad things, but sometimes the cops are right. You can't judge by just a uniform. You have to judge by what the person *does*. And I agree with him." Kate swallowed hard. "I mean Derek and me never dated because of color or anything. Or politics. I dated him because he was smart. And successful. And generous. And really, incredibly organized," she mused, temporarily losing track of her point. "But in the end it didn't work out," she shared, her breaths sounding shallow. "'Cause he decided that,--... I don't know." Kate flapped her arms in the wind as if looking for something to brace herself. "He just decided that he didn't want me anymore, is all. Started dating someone else."

As Jim suspected they would, Kate's eyes had begun to fill with tears. He reached a hand out to wipe them away, but Kate pushed his hand back.

"I'm fine," she combated. Then, thinking back to the time when she and Derek had first met, Kate corrected her previous statement. "You know what, that's not why I dated Derek, not at first." She wiped a tear away angrily. "I met him while I was working at an animal shelter." Kate smiled faintly. "He was really good with the animals. And then right when he was leaving, he dropped like a hundred dollar donation into the donor box." Kate rolled her eyes. "I thought he was so cool for doing that. Especially with the shelter always in threat of being closed down." She sniffed. "So when he came back with his friend the next day to take a stray home, I was already totally smitten." Kate wiped her nose and bit her lip uneasily.

Jim nodded, feeling very ready to take Kate in his arms to comfort her. Her eyes looked puffy and reddened. Her posture looked oddly slumped.

"So that, too," Kate told him. "You should remember that If you spend months and months dating someone, that person will start to believe that the relationship is *going* somewhere. So when it doesn't, that hurts. And the least you can do is tell them what they did wrong, or why you're just not calling anymore." Kate looked up into Jim's eyes. "How you break up with someone *matters*."

"Kate," Jim interrupted, "I know I said it before. But I really am sorry."

"It's alright," Kate grumbled. She waved goodbye to him weakly and turned back to her parents house.

"No I mean it," Jim insisted. Stepping close to her, he confessed, "I shouldn't have let it happen with Max. But honestly," he paused to breathe deeply, "I didn't even know how to stop it."

Kate searched over Jim's face, taking in his pained expressions.

"I've just been really embarrassed. And ashamed," he confessed. "I don't do one night stands. I'm not that guy. And I spend time second guessing myself. Like was I no good in bed, or did I do something wrong? Was I not funny enough?" Jim gritted his teeth as he dared to share his feelings of insecurity. "Mostly, I feel like I'm probably the most ordinary guy that ever lived. Like, there's literally, *zero* things special about me. So I'll be honest, I probably feel about you, the way you felt about that guy Derek."

Kate huffed as Jim continued. He touched the edge of her hair, admiring the satiny feel of it.

"No, I mean it. I *know* you're out of my league," he confessed. "Stylish and professional." He paused to share another point, "Please consider the fact that the thing with Max happened right when you and I had kind of just met. And I didn't know if you and I would go anywhere. Never thought that we'd -you know, *connect*."

Kate nodded and whispered, "Yeah I get it."

"Kate I swear," he started, "If there's any way possible that we could try again. I swear on my life, I will never, ever even look at another girl again. As long as we're together."

Kate snorted and shook her head. "I don't think so Jim. I mean, I wish I could say yes. But no. I'd be lying if I said I saw a way forward."

Jim stood still and waited for a few long seconds, hoping that Kate would change her mind or say something different. He kicked the ground with his boot, crunching the salt on the porch, giving her more moments to reconsider.

"Well," he said finally, then paused again, waiting.

Kate looked away toward her parents door, and waited for Jim to leave. She didn't enjoy this part of relationships, the breaking up and saying goodbye. It was awkward, painful. But at least she had the guts to face him and end it.

Jim leaned down carefully and placed a tender, tiny kiss on Kate's cheek. "Take care of yourself," he choked out, feeling more tearful than he'd imagined he would. In his heart of hearts, he had expected for Kate to forgive him, to give him a second chance.

"You too," she said, feeling confident that she was making the right choice. She felt there had been enough second chances for enough guys who had broken a woman's heart.

Jim strolled to his truck slowly, solemnly, his back turned to Kate. He stopped as he felt something in his pocket. To Kate's chagrin, when he turned around, Jim was wearing Kate's fuzzy purple mask.

"Oh my gosh, gimme that!" Kate said, chuckling despite herself.

Kate's steps sounded determined as they crunched through the snow. She attempted to take the mask from his hand only to find it dangling over her head in Jim's hand, just out of her reach.

"Don't be a jerk!" She sneered, jumping slightly to reach the mask. She didn't want to play his game, but she couldn't resist the challenge.

Jim chuckled as he stood to his tiptoes to keep the mask away from her. "Don't be so short!" he countered, enjoying the feel of Kate's closeness.

Kate continued to jump for a few more seconds, slapping Jim on the chest occasionally, demanding her mask.

Afraid that she would become genuinely angry, Jim conceded, "Alright here you go." He gently handed the mask over to Kate, who placed it promptly on her face. She stood there for a moment, allowing him to observe the mask in its full, purple glory.

Jim chuckled. The fur-lined purple velour seemed even more ridiculous in the sunlight. Staring into her eyes, his voice was warm and tender. "If I find more of your things in my truck, I'll come here to drop them off, or meet you at your apartment,--*wherever*. I'll find my way to where you are."

Kate shrugged nonchalantly, but nodded in agreement. She made small deliberate steps back to the house, leaving Jim at his truck,--hoping he'd find more things that belonged to sweet Kate.

The End

ABOUT THE AUTHOR

Kennedy Rockefeller lives with her one husband, her five beautiful children and three imaginary goldfish. She enjoys eating chocolate and taking frequent naps. She resides on Terra Firma with roughly 7.5 billion other humanoids. She is a Christian and enjoys a really good bargain. She has been known to use coupons. She would like her readers to know that should something unfortunate happen to any of the fictional characters in her novel, *Tyke did it*.

9 798575 650164